"Right now you have to worry about locating and deactivating that charm." Zelda looked at the clock. "In the next hour and ten minutes."

"Well, I know that Jason Richards had it fifteen minutes ago—" Sabrina jumped to her feet in a panic. "But he left the building!"

"Any guesses as to where he might have gone?" Hilda asked.

Struggling to stay calm, Sabrina tried to remember if Jason had said anything during the day that might give her a hint. He hadn't. But I did! "The Slicery. I told him I was playing in the Foosball tourna—"

Mr. Kraft's voice suddenly boomed beyond the closed conference room door. "You're *trying* to push the limits of my patience, aren't you?"

"Yes, absolutely," a familiar voice chirped.

Sabrina's heart lurched. "Oh no! Mr. Kraft found the duplicate I made to serve my detention!"

Sabrina, the Teenage Witch™ books

Available from ARCHWAY Paperbacks

Lotsa Luck

Diana G. Gallagher

AN ARCHWAY PAPERBACK
Published by POCKET BOOKS
New York London Toronto Sydney Tokyo Singapore

AN ARCHWAY PAPERBACK *Original*

An Archway Paperback published by
POCKET BOOKS, a division of Simon & Schuster Inc.
1230 Avenue of the Americas, New York, NY 10020

ISBN: 0-671-01980-5

First Archway Paperback printing May 1998

10 9 8 7 6 5 4 3 2 1

Printed in the U.S.A.

For Kristin Janschewitz
with affection

Lotsa Luck

Chapter 1

☆

☆

"Seven-thirteen! In the morning?" Shocked, Sabrina sat bolt upright in the comfortable easy chair in the turret alcove.

Lying on the bed, Salem casually opened one eye and gazed out the window. "Sun's rising in the east. Yep. It's morning."

"Why didn't you wake me, Salem?" As Sabrina jumped up, the textbook she had been studying before nodding off at midnight fell on the floor with a definitive thud. She was instantly awake and panicking.

"Do I *look* like an alarm clock?" A warlock convicted of plotting world domination and sentenced to being a cat for a hundred years, Salem yawned, stretched, then curled up to go back to sleep.

"No, but *that* can be arranged." Picking up the history book and tossing it on the bed, Sabrina impaled the cat with an icy stare as he suddenly came to attention.

"Got up on the wrong side of the chair, did you?" Arching his back, Salem stretched again, then settled into a sitting position and fluffed his sleep-matted fur with his tongue.

"There's no right side of *anything* this morning!" Frantic and annoyed, Sabrina gathered the spiral notebooks, pens, and books scattered around the floor and piled them on the bed by the history book.

"You think you've got problems? I was trying to decide which can of caviar to sample when you woke me up!" Salem sighed. "The dream is gone, but the craving lingers on."

"Can it, cat!" Turning toward the mirror, Sabrina grimaced at her rumpled condition and pointed. A split second later she was freshly showered and dressed. She allowed herself another second to contemplate the jeans, white blouse with pointy collar and cuffs, tailored forest green jacket, and ankle boots. Passing her own muster, she immediately darted across the room and began rummaging through her chest of drawers.

"So. What seems to be the problem *today?*" Salem flinched as clothes flew and drawers banged open and closed.

Moving on to the spell ingredients and paraphernalia piled on the window table and strewn around the floor, Sabrina ranted, "I only read three pages out of thirty about the Battle of Gettysburg and I've got a test second period! My English report on *The Yearling* is due this afternoon, and I haven't finished reading that book, either!"

"Well, pardon me for stating the obvious, but whose fault is that?" Salem ducked to avoid a cork-stoppered cask of sun-dried bats' feet Sabrina hurled over her shoulder.

Whirling, Sabrina looked at him narrowly and shook her finger in his startled face. "There are worse fates than being turned into an alarm clock, Salem."

"True." Whiskers twitching nervously, Salem asked another cautious question. "But would you mind explaining *why* you're mad at me before you cast a spell we'll *both* probably regret?"

Blinking, Sabrina lowered the lethal weapon that looked like an ordinary finger and sighed. "Sorry, Salem. I'm not mad at you at all. I'm mad at myself. And the world!"

"Well, I'm glad we got that cleared up." Lying down, Salem sighed with relief. "Anything I can do to help?"

"I doubt it." Sinking into the chair, Sabrina glanced over the chaotic disarray of miscellaneous mundane and magic stuff tossed and heaped around the room. "You can't work for me at the school rummage sale this afternoon so I can go to the Slicery."

"Well, I could, but I don't think your school or your customers are ready for a talking cat with a slick sales pitch. How'd you get roped into selling junk to garage-sale stalking bargain hunters in the first place?"

Sabrina threw up her hands. "I didn't know I'd be a finalist in the Slicery Foosball tournament when I volunteered! I mean, it never even occurred to me to try a fortune-telling spell to make sure my calendar was clear today!"

"Wouldn't have helped anyway," Salem said sagely. "The intrinsic problem with fortune-telling spells is that the future changes just because it's been observed."

Scowling thoughtfully, Sabrina aimed her finger at the bed. "The winner of the Foosball tournament gets twelve free pizzas and two tickets to the Leopard Spots concert."

"Leopard Spots?" Salem's eye warily followed the girl's finger. "That has a nice ring to it."

"It's also Harvey's favorite alternative group. He didn't make the cut in the first Foosball round because some joker bumped into him and spoiled his block. He's totally bummed."

"A calamity of such Earth-shaking proportions would ruin anybody's week," the cat said drolly. He cringed as Sabrina closed her eyes and began to intone a spell.

> *"Clothes and stuff in disarray, quickly put yourselves away!"*

Sabrina watched intently as everything strewn around the room began to sort, fold, and return itself to its proper place. Her dark frown deepened as the last shirt hung itself on a hanger and the closet door closed. "Blast! What did I do with that?"

"With what?" Rising, Salem peered over the edge of the bed as Sabrina bent down to look under it.

"Aunt Hilda's favorite pestle."

Salem sat back, his eyes widening. "You mean the oak one with ivy vines etched on the handle?"

"That's the one. I sorta borrowed it to practice grinding spell ingredients because I couldn't find mine." Moving to the window, Sabrina checked behind the curtains. Her own pestle was lying on the window sill. "Aunt Hilda's been in such a foul mood since she stormed home from her date with Mr. Kraft last Sunday, I don't dare not find it! She'll kill me!"

"I'm hungry. Gotta go!"

Leaping onto the floor, Salem was out the door and gone before Sabrina glanced back. Sighing, she put the plain pine pestle Aunt Zelda had given her with the crocks and jars of ground and unground magic makings now neatly arranged on the window table. With luck, the elegant oak pestle would turn up before Aunt Hilda wanted to use it.

And, Sabrina thought as she crossed to the far side of the bed and opened the top drawer of her chest, *if I get really lucky, all the questions on the American History test would only refer to the three pages I read last night or to the things I heard in class.* If her luck held, she'd also be able to skim the rest of *The Yearling* and dash off an acceptable report during fourth period study hall and lunch. Then to top things off, someone would agree to work her shift at the rummage sale so she wouldn't forfeit the Slicery Foosball tournament as a "no-show." The Leopard Spots concert had been sold-out for weeks and Harvey desperately wanted to go. Whether or not he could attend depended entirely on whether or not she won the tournament.

Sighing again, Sabrina rummaged through a box of trinkets and jewelry looking for something to add a bit of sparkle to her wardrobe. Her gaze fell on a pink rabbit's foot keychain she had won at a carnival when she was six. Inspiration struck with staggering, forehead-slapping force.

Luck was obviously the key to solving all the problems of the day, and she was a witch! Can someone *make* luck? Pulling her huge, leather-bound and jewel-inlaid magic book out from under the bed, Sabrina checked the index and grinned.

"Lucky charm. That should do it!"

Although she was a skilled Foosball player, it couldn't hurt to have a hefty dose of good luck working for her in the playoffs. And she definitely needed an edge if she hoped to pass her history test and finish her English report.

Flipping the book open to the correct page, Sabrina glanced at the list of ingredients: *A depository for the luck.*

"That's easy enough." Grabbing the pink rabbit's foot from the drawer, Sabrina perched on the edge of the bed and read the directions. With the furry foot in her left hand she closed her eyes and recited the incantation, filling in the blanks with the appropriate words.

> *"Pink, furry foot with keychain gold, good fortune for the bearer hold. When circumstances run amok, dispel the bad with lotsa luck."*

Sabrina started as a tickling warmth generated by the furry foot seeped into her hand. However, she kept her grip tightened until the heat had been completely absorbed through her skin and the simmering charm cooled.

Then she noticed the fine print at the bottom of the page, which was—as usual—impossible to read without a magnifying device. Since the fine print almost, but not always, contained information vital to a witch's well-being regarding the relevant spell, Sabrina raised her finger to point up a magnifying glass so she could read the text. She paused as Aunt Hilda's magically amplified voice filled the room.

"Sabrina! Have you seen my etched oak pestle anywhere?"

Oops!

Wincing, Sabrina glanced at the pink rabbit's foot. If her spell had worked and the carnival doo-dad was *really* loaded with good luck, then Aunt Hilda's pestle would turn up before she had to admit she had borrowed and misplaced it.

If the charm didn't work, the sooner she knew, the better off she'd be.

"Better hurry, Sabrina!" Aunt Zelda called from the hallway. "Or you'll be late for school."

"On my way!" Stuffing the rabbit's foot in her small shoulder bag, Sabrina glanced at the fine print.

"Sabrina!" There was a dangerous edge of irritation in Aunt Hilda's amplified voice now. "Salem just told me you borrowed my pestle! Would you bring it back, please!"

Frowning, Sabrina closed the magic book. Tearing the notes she had managed to take on the first three pages of the history chapter out of a spiral notebook, she folded and stuffed them in her bag so she could review them between classes. After picking up her books, she dashed for the door. But before leaving, she paused to scan the room. Aunt Hilda's favorite pestle did not suddenly appear from wherever it was hiding.

Maybe my luck spell hasn't worked after all, Sabrina thought glumly as she sprinted for the stairs. *In which case, reading the fine print isn't necessary. . . .*

Chapter 2

☆

☆

Frowning as she paused in the kitchen doorway, Sabrina listened to the traitorous, tattletale Salem shamelessly beg Aunt Hilda for caviar.

"The craving is driving me crazy," the cat wailed plaintively. "And it's all Sabrina's fault."

"My fault?" Sabrina blurted out.

Looking up with surprise, Salem didn't miss a beat. "Because you woke me up before I had a taste."

"That was a dream!" Sabrina protested.

"So?" Curling into a ball on the counter, Salem groaned. "I'm going into caviar withdrawal."

"You'll get over it." Standing behind the island counter wearing the apron she had won for honorable mention at the Witch's Chili Cook-Off ten years ago, Aunt Hilda acknowledged her niece with a curt nod. "Sabrina."

Sabrina returned Aunt Hilda's annoyed glance

with a tight, sheepish smile. All the drawers and cabinets were open and a large percentage of the contents had been thrown on the floor. Her aunt obviously hadn't found the missing oak pestle yet.

And her bad mood hadn't improved, either.

"I don't mind your borrowing my things, Sabrina, but I'd really appreciate it if you'd put them back where they belong." Dish towels, silverware, pots, pans, and plastic storage containers suddenly flew back into place as Hilda swept her pointed finger over the mess.

"I'm sorry, Aunt Hilda." Casting a glance at the cat, who was moaning dramatically and avoiding her gaze, Sabrina shifted uncomfortably. "It won't happen again. I promise."

"Okay." Aunt Hilda's eyes widened expectantly as she held out her hand for the pestle.

Cornered and guilty and without a clue as to where the elusive pestle was, Sabrina was about to confess that she had lost it when her aunt Zelda rammed into her. Stumbling to the side, Sabrina grunted as her bag slipped off her shoulder and fell on the floor with her books.

Blinded by the towering pile of old clothes she was carrying, Aunt Zelda stopped dead. "Oh, Sabrina! I'm so sorry. Are you all right?"

"I'm fine." Stooping to pick up her things, Sabrina reached for a pen that had rolled under the table.

"What's with all those clothes, Zelda?" Hilda asked.

"They're our donation to the rummage sale at Sabrina's school today."

Startled, Sabrina looked up. "That's great, Aunt Zelda, but I don't have time to take them to the gym!"

"Don't worry, Sabrina. I'll drive them over later this morning." Zelda bent slightly to catch a red, silk blouse that was slipping off the top of the stack. "Point these over to the door for me, will you, Hilda? If I raise my finger, they'll all be on the floor."

Relieved, Sabrina smiled. Maybe her lucky charm wasn't a total washout. Aside from not having to take precious time to donate the clothes personally, she hadn't been questioned by her aunts as to why she couldn't. They would not be pleased to learn she had procrastinated herself into a bind with her schoolwork.

Rolling her eyes, Hilda yanked the bundle of clothes out of Zelda's arms with a deft point and dropped them in a tangled heap by the door. "Why didn't you just point them down here in the first place?"

"Because every once in a while I like to remind myself how difficult life can be for mortals. It reinforces my respect for them." Blowing a stray wisp of hair off her face, Zelda exhaled wearily and sank into a chair by the table. "I don't know how they ever get anything done without the benefit of magic."

Sabrina's smile broadened as her gaze flicked from the clothes to the back of the table where the

11

pen had rolled. Aunt Hilda's oak pestle was lying in the corner.

Another stroke of good luck! And all because her aunt had bumped into her, which had only happened because Aunt Zelda was on one of her periodic manual-instead-of-magic-labor kicks. If the pen hadn't rolled out of reach, she would never have looked behind the table for Aunt Hilda's pestle.

Salem must have rolled the pestle from her room and lost track of it when something more enticing distracted him, Sabrina surmised as she reached for the antique wooden tool. Although he was a warlock who had been stripped of his powers and locked in a cat's body, Salem's nature was totally feline. Grabbing the pestle, Sabrina stood up.

Salem raised his head and blinked. "Found it, huh?"

"No thanks to you," Sabrina hissed as she pointed it into her aunt's outstretched hand. "Here you go, Aunt Hilda."

"Thanks." Catching the pestle, Hilda trudged to the farside of the counter. "Life has gotten depressing enough lately. I just couldn't face cooking without my favorite pestle, too."

"What happened between you and Mr. Kraft anyway?" Zelda asked.

"Nothing I care to discuss. Willard"—Hilda grimaced, as though choking on the vice-principal's name—"is history. And I could care less."

"Then how come you're so depressed, Aunt Hilda?" Sitting down at the table, Sabrina pointed and a jelly-filled doughnut appeared in front of her.

"The definitive lack of *charming* male company comes to mind." Gripping the pestle, Hilda whacked a small, brown nutmeg resting on the cutting board.

Salem jumped as one of the pieces rocketed in front of his nose. "Who declared this attack-the-cat day?"

"Sorry, Salem." Hilda whacked the remaining pieces a second time for good measure. "I'll make it up to you if and when I ever get happy again."

"Meaning I can't expect to find caviar in my dish until you find Mr. Right?" Salem drooped. "I'll never eat fish eggs again."

"You're not whipping up another man-dough date, are you?" Zelda leaned back and looked at Hilda askance. "You've already had three this month!"

"No." Hilda scraped the crushed nutmeg into a wooden bowl and picked up the pestle. "Developing a meaningful and lasting relationship simply isn't possible with a man who has a life expectancy of four hours."

Zelda smiled. "Considering some of the dates we've cooked up, a four-hour limit does have certain advantages."

"I suppose." Scowling, Hilda smashed and ground the innocent spice. "But as much as I'd like a little *genuine* romance in my life right now, a man-dough man just won't cut it. There's no element of anticipation or surprise when the personality traits are baked to order." Hilda sighed despondently.

"That's not always true." Resting her chin in her hands, Aunt Zelda heaved a sigh that was heavier, longer, and more bummed out than Hilda's. "My man-dough recipes don't always produce the results I anticipate."

Taking a bite of the doughnut, Sabrina chewed as she recalled the man-dough date she had made when Harvey had accepted Libby's invitation to a school dance last year. Chad, the man-dough date, was so totally enthusiastic and attentive, he was boring. On the other hand, Harvey had kept her on the brink of delicious anxiety for months before he had finally gotten up the nerve to express his feelings. She knew exactly what Aunt Hilda was talking about.

Grinding and smashing with her cherished oak pestle, Hilda fumed. "There's just no substitute for the excitement and unpredictability of an encounter with the real thing!"

Which, Sabrina thought, was really curious. Her aunt's unpredictable, sometimes stormy and sometimes sweet relationship with the dreaded Mr. Kraft fulfilled all those requirements. Although she didn't like him, Sabrina had been hoping Aunt Hilda and the vice-principal would work things out. He had been just as cantankerous and hard to get along with as her angry aunt all week. And *that* always spelled trouble for her.

"Don't I know it," Zelda mumbled.

Hilda glanced at Zelda curiously. "Don't tell me you're suffering from man deprivation, too."

"Not a chance." Zelda scoffed. "I've got a severe case of lost reference book blues."

"You're pining for a lost book?" Arching an eyebrow, Sabrina regarded Aunt Zelda skeptically. A scientific genius who had kept pace with every new theory, development, and breakthrough over the past several centuries, Zelda was as knowledge-able about modern physics as she was about ancient magic. But sometimes her perspective totally eluded Sabrina's comprehension.

"Dr. Peavey's Basic Principles of Science," Zelda said. "I've contacted every rare book dealer in the world and there simply isn't a copy to be found on the planet!"

"Maybe because Albert Einstein's theory of relativity made that musty old textbook obsolete." Hilda grunted with the effort of grinding bits of nutmeg into a fine powder by hand. "None of it made any sense to me *before* Einstein."

"Why can't you just use a spell to conjure a copy, Aunt Zelda?" Sabrina asked, puzzled. "It's just an old book—"

"Not that anyone would notice." Setting the oak pestle aside, Hilda pointed at an empty mug and magically filled it with steaming hot chocolate. Then she threw in a pinch of the nutmeg she had so rigorously ground by hand. Picking up her mug,

Hilda joined them at the table. "It's been over a hundred and fifty years since *Peavey's* was the last word in science, Zelda."

Sabrina took another bite of doughnut and shook her head, fascinated by how her aunts combined mortal and magic methods on whims that defied reason.

"But it was used in every school in the country. You'd think someone *somewhere* would have a copy, wouldn't you?" Zelda eyed the mug of hot chocolate Hilda placed on the table. "Didn't you make some for everyone?"

"Oh. Sorry." Casually flicking her finger, Hilda zapped up two more mugs of hot chocolate.

"What? No nutmeg?" Sabrina frowned.

Hilda pointed at the bowl of ground nutmeg. Zelda and Sabrina held up their mugs to catch the two small streams of powder that zoomed toward them.

"Oh, fine." Salem grumbled. "They get nutmeg and I get zip. Thanks a lot. All *I* want is a little dish of caviar."

"Remember that the next time you're plotting to take over the world, Salem," Hilda said.

Sabrina was about to suggest that her aunts might benefit from a couple of lucky charms when she glanced at the wall clock and noticed the time. Popping the last piece of doughnut into her mouth, she jumped up. "I'm late! Gotta go."

"Just tell whoever's in charge of the rummage sale that I'll have our donation there before noon."

"Libby's in charge of the rummage sale, Aunt Zelda. I try to avoid her!"

Quickly gathering the books and bag that were still lying on the floor, Sabrina dashed out the door. Confident that her lucky charm would somehow delay the bus's arrival so she wouldn't miss it, she raced for the corner.

She arrived just as the bus pulled away from the curb and accelerated down the street without her.

Chapter 3

☆

☆

Shrugging as she watched the bus turn onto Elm, Sabrina simply popped herself to Westbridge High. It was still early and the rest room was empty. Contrary to how it might seem, missing the bus had actually been another lucky coincidence. Now she had a whole half-hour to skim the chapter on the Battle of Gettysburg before her first period math class.

Heading out into the hall, Sabrina went directly to her locker and dumped everything except her history, math, and chemistry books, a spiral notebook, and her shoulder bag inside. As she turned to head to the library, she collided with Jason Richards. Her chemistry book fell on the floor.

"Oh, gosh, I'm sorry!" Squatting down to retrieve it, Sabrina looked up to find herself nose to nose with the boy.

A junior and a total hunk with sandy brown hair and piercing brown eyes, Jason was new at Westbridge High. Smart, athletic, and pleasant, he had become instantly popular. He had also developed an instant interest in Sabrina that was flattering and unsettling at the same time. The demands of her school activities and magic studies to get her witch's license had forced her to stop going steady with Harvey. Under the influence of a no-pain spell delivered in a cup of butterscotch pudding, he had accepted the idea of a nonexclusive relationship. That had hurt, but although her heart still belonged to Harvey, having the freedom to date others had made life infinitely more exciting.

And Jason was an intriguing other.

"Don't be sorry, Sabrina." Grinning, Jason handed her the book. "I just love running into you like this."

"I think I'm the one who's doing the running into," Sabrina said as she started to rise. A tingling that registered only slightly below Harvey's number ten tingle on her personal reaction scale tickled her skin as Jason grasped her hand to help her up. "Thanks."

"You're welcome."

Smiling, Sabrina indulged herself with a few seconds of staring into Jason's gorgeous eyes.

"Sabrina, there's something I want—"

"Sabrina!" Harvey's voice rang out from the end of the corridor. "Man, am I glad I found—"

Sabrina's heart lurched as Harvey skidded to a stop, spying Jason.

"Sorry." Harvey waved stiffly and shifted awkwardly. "I'll, uh—catch ya later."

"Harvey! Wait!" Ducking around Jason, Sabrina started after Harvey as he turned and disappeared down the adjacent hall.

Having the advantage of proximity at the moment, Jason fell into step beside her. "If you're not busy next weekend, I was wondering—"

"Later, okay, Jason?" Quickening her pace, Sabrina shrugged apologetically as she moved ahead of him. "I've got to cram a whole night's studying for my history test into twenty-five minutes. Bye!" Without waiting for a response, Sabrina ran around the corner.

Harvey was nowhere to be seen, but Libby barged in the door at the end of the hallway. Not in the mood for a confrontation with the undisputed boss of anything and everything involving the junior class, Sabrina did an about-face.

And found herself sandwiched between Libby, the impending storm, and Valerie, her new, socially inept, anxiety-ridden friend. Val's unrequited aspirations to be popular were annoying, but she shared with Sabrina the dubious distinction of being on Libby's "weirdo freak" list. Even though Sabrina's precious study minutes were ticking by, she couldn't abandon Val to engage the class tyrant alone. With luck, Libby would just storm on by without acknowledging their lowly presences.

"Hi, Sabrina." A lukewarm smile flicked across Val's face as she pushed a lock of straight brown hair behind her ear.

"What's the matter?" Sabrina asked with genuine concern. Valerie's problems were usually superficial in the cosmic scope of things, but always of monumental importance to her.

"Would you believe that Libby forgot to schedule me to work the rummage sale?" Depressed by the implied rejection, Valerie sagged. "I mean, how am I ever going to get *anywhere* at Westbridge if Libby won't even let me sell old clothes."

"No problem!" Sabrina grinned, amazed at how her lucky charm could turn an apparently dismal twist of fate into a fortuitous event. "I've been trying to find someone to work—"

Valerie's face brightened as her gaze drifted down the corridor. "Looks like Libby's got a major mad going. Maybe I can help! Then she might realize I'm not the dweeb she thinks I am. Even though I am."

"No, Val. I don't think that's a good—"

"Hey! Libby!" Valerie waved. "How's it going?"

Sabrina winced, wondering if the fine print she hadn't read was a warning about the charm's luck limit. As Libby came to an abrupt halt beside them, she was certain hers had just run out.

"Badly, if you must know!"

Ignoring the cheerleader's angry glare, Val pressed ahead. "What's wrong?"

Sabrina glanced through an open classroom door at the clock above the chalkboard. She still had almost twenty minutes, but for some unfathomable reason, Libby had decided not to brush Valerie off with a single caustic comment and move on as usual.

"Benjamin Heller is home sick today, so I'm one salesperson short for the rummage sale."

Valerie spoke up before Sabrina could stop her. "I'll do it, Libby. I signed up, but you must have missed my name when you made up the schedule."

"I don't *miss* anything," Libby snapped. "However, since I'm in a bind, I'll make an exception for you this time. Be in the gym at three o'clock sharp. Or I guarantee you'll never work another charity event at this school again."

"I'll be there!" Beaming, Valerie hugged her books to her chest.

Sabrina groaned inwardly as the one and only candidate she had found to substitute for her at the rummage sale after school was snatched away along with her hope of getting Leopard Spots concert tickets.

"Now, if you'll excuse me," Libby said, "I've got to go panic about my driver's test sixth period. It's my second try and if I don't pass, I'll flunk Driver's Ed."

"I could help you at lunch." On a roll, Valerie foolishly flung herself into the path of Libby's contempt. "My dad came up with a really neat system for practicing without a car—"

"I'd rather fail." Rudely cutting Valerie off, Libby stalked away.

Valerie's magic moment of in-crowd acceptance burst with the disdainful dismissal and she sighed with stoic resignation, then brightened. "Well, at least we'll be working together this afternoon, Sabrina."

"Yeah. Guess so. Look, I've got to get to the library now, Val. See you second period."

"Okay." Preoccupied with Libby's dislike, Val walked away psyching herself. "There's got to be *something* I can do to make her like me."

Sabrina dashed for the stairs.

"No running in the halls, Ms. Spellman!"

The sound of Vice-Principal Kraft's stern voice had the effect of turning Sabrina's leather boots to cement. She stopped and looked back with an apologetic smile. "Sorry. I was just on my way to the library."

"Then there's no reason to rush." Mr. Kraft's brow knit in consternation and his mustache twitched as he folded his hands in front of him. "Last time I checked all the books were waiting patiently on the shelves. They'll still be there if it takes you an extra thirty seconds to—*walk!*"

"Yes, sir." Sabrina nodded agreeably. Her study time was quickly dwindling and she didn't want to trigger a lengthy review about proper deportment in the corridors of Westbridge High. Unfortunately, Mr. Kraft didn't need an excuse to detain her or expound.

"As I recall, Ms. Spellman, I've had to remind you to slow down on more than one occasion.

Since you obviously need more than a verbal reminder—"

Desperate, Sabrina pointed past his shoulder and gasped. "Look!"

"What?" Mr. Kraft looked back as a fire extinguisher fell from its unlatched holder and crashed to the floor.

Carbon-dioxide foam spewed from the nozzle as Sabrina activated the mechanism with another deft point. As the vice-principal took off down the hall to investigate, Sabrina spun on her heels and ran up the stairs. Ten minutes of studying with the aid of a speed-reading spell just might be enough to get her through her American history exam with a passing grade.

Slowing to a walk as she entered the school's sanctuary of books and quiet, Sabrina headed for a remote corner to hide before anyone else decided this was the ideal moment for a casual conversation. Mr. Pool, her biology teacher from last year, was sitting at the long table in the reference section. He looked up as she emerged from two rows of towering bookcases. Judging by the hangdog scowl on his face, he was not happy, either.

"Sorry," Sabrina whispered. "I didn't mean to interrupt. I'll just go over here and—"

"Life is too short, Sabrina."

"For what?"

"To waste time chasing foolish dreams of literary fame and fortune. Or anything else that remotely smacks of artistic achievement." Sighing, the teacher raised a nine-by-twelve manila envelope and started to rip it in half. The numerous sheets of paper inside it refused to be so unceremoniously destroyed and successfully resisted his efforts.

"Uh-huh. Okay!" Sabrina backed away.

"Do you know what this is?" Mr. Pool held up a letter he had taken out of the envelope.

Trapped, Sabrina shrugged. "No. What?"

"The final page of an illustrious, science-fiction writing career that never happened, that's what." He shook his head in disgusted dismay as he scanned the paper. "It's not even an editorial rejection about my story specifically. It's a form letter!"

"You write stories, Mr. Pool?" Sabrina asked, surprised. "You mean about aliens and UFOs and stuff?"

"There's more to science fiction than aliens and UFOs, Sabrina. But, yes. I've been writing and rewriting *The Tachyon Terror* for years." Wadding up the rejection letter, Mr. Pool heaved it across the room. "I just can't sell it!"

"Gosh, I'm so sorry. I—"

Rising, Mr. Pool smiled weakly. "Don't be sorry, Sabrina. Maybe it's time I faced the fact that I'm a creative washout. A wannabe author who'll never have a chance to be a has-been. After all, there are worse fates than being a lousy writer with no sense of style, characterization, or plot who's doomed to teach biology to a bunch of kids who could care less about mitosis for the rest of his life. Although at the moment, I can't think of what. But thanks for listening."

Stunned, Sabrina stared after the depressed teacher as he trudged off to his first period class. Mr. Pool along with Libby and most of her friends all seemed to need a little bit of luck today. Unfortunately, she had only made one lucky charm and she needed it to keep her grade average from slipping below the acceptable percentage her aunts had set. Sighing, Sabrina pulled out a chair and prepared to point a double-fast, speed reading spell over herself when yet another incensed voice interrupted.

"We have trash cans, Sabrina!"

Snapping her head around, Sabrina met the librarian's disappointed stare with one of blank confusion. An attractive, helpful, and normally pleasant woman of thirty, Ms. Whitman was holding the wadded-up rejection notice Mr. Pool had discarded. "That's not mine, Ms. Whitman."

Scowling, the librarian unfolded the paper. Her expression slowly changed from displeasure to intrigued curiosity as she read the notice aloud. " 'We regret to inform you that your submission does not meet our needs at this time. Burt Cassidy, editor. *Tales of Space and Time.*'" She glanced back at Sabrina with a puzzled frown. "Whose is it?"

"Mr. Pool's."

"Mr. Pool writes science fiction?"

"Apparently." Spotting the manila envelope the biology teacher had left on the table, Sabrina picked it up and handed it to the librarian. "This is the story the magazine turned down."

Ms. Whitman eagerly took the envelope and pulled out the manuscript. *"The Tachyon Terror.* Hmmm." A mischievous sparkle lit up her dark brown eyes. "Maybe someone else should read this. A second opinion can't hurt and I love this stuff."

"Well, Mr. Pool *did* leave it behind," Sabrina said, nodding. Getting the librarian's approval wouldn't help Mr. Pool sell the story, but it might inspire him to keep trying.

After tucking the envelope under her arm, Ms. Whitman glanced at the rejection letter again as she returned to her desk. "Burt Cassidy—"

Alone at last, Sabrina set her books on the table. And the five-minute bell before first period rang.

Chapter 4

☆

Want another one?" Hilda raised her finger to refill Zelda's mug with hot chocolate.

"No, thanks." Zelda waved the offer aside. "Three's my limit and it's not helping."

"No, it isn't, is it? Usually chocolate in any form makes me feel better when I'm depressed." Hilda frowned into her empty mug and set it down. "But not today. I suppose I could add a pinch of happy horntoad extract to give it a little more punch."

"But the effect is so fleeting, it's not worth the trouble." Rising, Zelda headed for the door.

Hilda nodded. A mood-altering potion wouldn't solve the real problem anyway. It would just make her forget about it for awhile. And after the effects wore off, she'd feel ten times more miserable than she did now.

"I'm going to check my E-mail, Hilda. I haven't

heard back from Harry's Used Book Emporium in Lima, Peru."

"Good luck."

"I could use some." Looking back over her shoulder, Zelda grinned. "It's too bad lucky charms are so fickle."

"Yeah. They're not worth the trouble, either," Hilda mumbled as Zelda left for the study and her portable computer.

"Lighten up." Swishing his tail, Salem glared at Hilda. "At least you're not a powerless cat with a caviar craving no one seems inclined to satisfy."

Hilda glared back and pointed the empty mugs into the dishwasher. "We can't always get what we want, Salem."

"We could if we moved to the Other Realm," the cat grumbled.

"We'd be bored to death within forty-eight hours if all our heart's desires could be fulfilled with a point. Sabrina didn't even last that long when she decided to stay with Vesta, remember?" To prove her point, Hilda stepped over to the island counter. Picking up the bowl of ground nutmeg, she carefully poured it through a funnel into a small jar. When all the powder was inside, she capped the jar, then pointed it onto the spice rack. "See? There's nothing like a little domestic drudgery to give one a sense of real accomplishment."

"Right. Except the backyard isn't exactly teeming with fish I can catch myself."

"You just have to be patient—"

"That is little consolation for a cat who desperately needs instant gratification," Salem huffed. "And I don't believe for one minute that you're just going to sit back and wait hundreds of years for the love of your life to ring the doorbell."

"At least I *have* hundreds of years." Grabbing a sponge off the sink, Hilda wandered back to the table to wipe it off. "Mortals only have a few decades. Considering the odds against them, the percentage of successful mortal matches is amazingly high."

"And in the meantime the cat starves." Growling softly, Salem flopped down on the counter and rested his chin on his front paws.

"You're hardly starving." Bending over to brush doughnut crumbs off Sabrina's chair, Hilda spotted a tuft of pink fur under the table. "Have you been hunting in the Other Realm, Salem?"

"Me?" The cat's head jerked up in alarm. "No way! Drell would condemn me to a fate infinitely worse than being a cat if he caught me stalking his precious moles and other furry friends!" Salem shuddered. "Besides, the mere thought of actually eating a pink mouse or a rainbow-striped rabbit makes me gag. Yech!"

"Then what's this?" Hilda pointed the furry pink thing into her hand.

"Never saw it before," Salem said. "Honest. As I recall, Drell's animals don't wear gold chains."

Taking a closer look and realizing the furry

thing was just a dime-store rabbit's foot key-chain, Hilda relaxed. Although she had some influence with Drell because of an old romance that had gone sour, she knew she wouldn't be able to stop the flamboyant warlock from getting revenge on anyone who dared harm a protected member of his critter collection. Salem could be a major pain, but she had grown fond of him since the Head of the Witch's Council had turned him into a cat and placed him in the Spellmans' custody.

"It must have fallen out of Sabrina's bag when she dropped it." Slipping the doodad into her apron pocket, Hilda pushed in the chair.

"Yeah." Salem yawned. "She was a bit frazzled and totally testy this morning."

"Really? I didn't notice. How come?"

"Nothing critical." Yawning again, Salem gave his paws a few idle grooming licks. "Just a test she didn't study for, a report she didn't write, and a Foosball tournament she isn't going to win because she has a conflicting obligation."

The doorbell rang.

"Would you get that, Hilda?" Zelda called from the study. "I'm in a rare books chat room waiting for a duke in Austria to check the castle library!"

"Why not?" Tossing the sponge back into the sink, Hilda headed toward the front door. "It's probably just someone trying to sell us something and I need a target for my frustrations!"

"Wait for me!" Salem leaped off the counter and padded along behind her. "A little magical sport at a mortal's expense might take my mind off my stomach."

Hilda paused with her hand on the doorknob and looked down at the expectant cat. "Nothing can take your mind off your stomach."

"Open the door," Salem said bluntly. "The suspense is killing me."

Expecting to find a five-foot-six, balding insurance salesman with glasses and crooked, yellow teeth standing on the porch, Hilda donned her most annoyed scowl and threw open the door. Her mouth fell open in speechless surprise.

Six feet of trim muscle wearing a white turtleneck and tweed sport jacket with jeans and boots topped off with dark hair met her astonished gaze with blazing blue eyes set in a ruggedly handsome, tanned face. The vision grinned, revealing perfect teeth, and spoke in a deep, melodious voice that made every nerve ending in her entire body vibrate.

"Sorry to bother you, ma'am, but—"

"Not ma'am, please," Hilda said breathlessly. "Hilda."

"Hilda. What a charming name." The stranger's warm smile widened. "I just got into town from Arizona last night and I don't know my way around yet. Can you tell me how to get to the university auditorium?"

Stunned by her unexpected and remarkable good

luck, Hilda reacted without hesitation. "Sure, but I'll have to write the directions down because it's kind of complicated. So you might as well come in and make yourself comfortable—what did you say your name was?"

"Gabe. Gabe Hawkins."

"Gabe." Grinning like a schoolgirl who had just been asked to her first dance, Hilda stepped back to let the man enter. The tangy scent of a masculine aftershave teased her as he stepped through the door.

Carrying a cello case!

"You play the cello?" Hilda asked inanely. "I play the violin!"

"Really?" Gabe's blazing blues blinked. "I just joined the university music department teaching staff and I'm supposed to meet with the school symphony conductor this afternoon at four."

"Then you've got lots of time, don't you?" Hilda held her breath, barely daring to hope. It was just going on ten.

Gabe nodded with a throaty chuckle. "Plenty. I can read the most intricate of musical orchestrations by sight, but I can't read a map to save myself. Which is why I decided to find the campus this morning. Unfortunately, I got hopelessly lost within the space of a few blocks."

Unfortunately nothing!

"Well, Gabe, you're in luck. I've got a pot of coffee brewing and a freshly baked batch of cinnamon rolls,"—casually pointing toward the kitchen, Hilda instantly created the desired items—"just begging for company."

As gorgeous Gabe closed his eyes to breathe in the tantalizing aromas of cinnamon and coffee, Hilda quickly slipped off her apron and dropped it on the foyer floor.

"Coffee, cinnamon rolls, and a charming companion." Gabe grinned with genuine pleasure. "A combination I cannot refuse."

"Cool." Hooking her arm under Gabe's, Hilda steered him toward the kitchen. Enchanted and thrilled by the spontaneous and apparently mutual rapport that had instantly sprung up between her and the handsome musician, she didn't interfere when Salem immediately pounced on the rabbit's foot that rolled out of the apron pocket.

Sabrina stared at the test lying on the desk in front of her in shock.

There was only one question.

Write an essay detailing why the Battle Of Gettysburg was the turning point in the War Between the States.

Sabrina didn't have a clue beyond the simple fact that the Union Army had won the engagement. The more complex and far-reaching consequences of the outcome was covered at the end of the fourth chapter, which she hadn't read. If the material had been discussed in class, she didn't remember.

Hoping that holding her lucky charm would jog

her memory, Sabrina reached into her bag and fumbled through the makeup, pens, and papers stuffed inside it. Nothing furry touched her groping hand. On the verge of panic, she dumped the contents on the floor.

The rabbit's foot wasn't there.

But the history teacher's attention was.

"Explain yourself, Sabrina. If you can."

"Explain?" Stricken, Sabrina sat up and searched Mr. Rathbone's brooding face for some evidence of compassionate understanding. Not a hint. "Explain what?"

"What you're doing, of course."

"Doing?" Sabrina shrugged slightly and smiled lamely. "Would you believe I was looking for my lucky rabbit's foot?"

"No, but—" Bending over, Mr. Rathbone picked up some folded sheets of spiral notebook paper and opened them. "I do believe you were looking for your cheat sheets."

Sabrina gasped as he held out the history notes she had put in her bag that morning. Failing the test was one thing. Being accused of cheating when she wasn't was even worse!

"Those are just my study notes. I wasn't—"

"Tell it to Mr. Kraft." Eyeing her with contempt, Mr. Rathbone nodded toward the door. "Now."

Libby and Jill snickered.

Harvey and Val both coughed with embarrassment.

Helpless to do anything but obey, Sabrina gathered her things and crept down the aisle amid muffled laughter and derisive whispers. When she came abreast of Harvey, she paused to look him in the eye.

Shaking his head, Harvey lowered his gaze.

"Cheater!" Libby hissed.

Cheeks flaming with humiliation, Sabrina fled into the hall.

Branded!

☆

Chapter 5

☆

Banzai!" Leaping on the furry foot, Salem grabbed it in his sharp feline teeth and tossed it over his head. *There are certain things no self-respecting cat can ignore,* he thought as he swiped at the toy with his paw and watched it career across the dining room floor. Furry pink things definitely fell into that category. As long as they weren't *alive* and pink and part of Drell's prized menagerie.

Hunkering down with his unwavering eye focused on the make-believe prey, Salem wiggled his haunches in anticipation, then sprang. Snagging the hapless furry thing in his mouth again, he threw it over his head.

Zelda caught it and tossed it back.

A prisoner of his feline nature, Salem sat on his haunches and batted the flying furry bit in midair. He yelled as he leaped and trapped it under clawed paws the instant it touched the ground. "Wahoo!"

"At least someone in this house is having a good time." Looking thoroughly disgruntled, Zelda dragged herself to the kitchen door.

"Better knock before entering," Salem warned.

"Why? Is Hilda trying to cook from scratch again?"

Salem chuckled. The last time Hilda had tried making dinner the mortal way, it had taken an hour of serious pointing to clean up the mess. "Well, let's just say she's cooking. Believe it or not, a sizzling romance with Mr. Right may be heating to the boiling point as we speak."

"You're kidding?" Zelda peeked around the doorjamb, then quickly jerked back. "You're not kidding! Where'd he come from?"

"Arizona. He got lost on his way to see the symphony conductor at the university and stopped here to ask directions. He plays the cello and teaches music." Salem cocked his head thoughtfully. "Quite a coincidence, wouldn't you say?"

"Yes. Quite a coincidence. I wish I was having the same luck finding *Dr. Peavey's Basic Principals of Science.*"

"The Austrian duke didn't have it in the castle library, huh?"

"No." Displeasure darkened Zelda's face as she shook her head. "I think he was just trying to keep me on-line hoping I'd donate to his castle preservation fund."

Jumping back suddenly, Salem poised on his hind feet for a few seconds, then whacked the furry foot across the room again. Bounding after it, he firmly clamped it in his mouth.

The back doorbell rang.

Lost in troubled thought, Zelda didn't move.

Salem trotted into the kitchen with his prize, but ignored the door when the bell rang a second time. He was a cat. He couldn't answer it.

Sitting at the table holding hands with Gabe, Hilda tore her gaze away from his and frowned at the back door. "Zelda!"

Zelda stepped into the doorway. "I'm right here, Hilda. You don't have to shout."

The bell rang again.

"Would you get that?" Hilda asked as her adoring eyes drifted back to Gabe. "And if it's another tall, dark, handsome stranger, tell him he's fifteen minutes too late."

"I just love a woman with a sense of humor," Gabe said.

Rolling her eyes, Zelda strode to the door and threw it open. "Yes?"

"Delivery for Salem Spellman care of Zelda Spellman."

For me? Salem looked up with sudden interest.

A man in uniform thrust a small cardboard box into Zelda's hands and held out a clipboard. "Sign here, please."

"Wait just a minute." Zelda held up a staying hand. "What's in this?"

The deliveryman shrugged. "Don't ask me, lady. I just deliver."

Zelda glanced at Salem. "Did you order something without telling me?"

Unable to speak in front of the mortal or meow with his mouth full of pink fur, Salem shook his head no.

Gabe laughed good-naturedly. "I talk to my dogs like I expect them to answer, too."

"Isn't that sweet, Zelda?"

"Charming." Zelda muttered as she scanned the package label. "Oh, my. I forgot I ordered this."

Curious because she had ordered whatever it was for *him,* Salem tried to drop the furry foot to investigate further and couldn't. The tip of his tooth was caught in the small hole in the metal keychain latch.

"Signature, ma'am?" The delivery man pressed the clipboard forward and left as soon as Zelda finished scribbling her name.

"So what's in it?" Hilda asked curiously.

Yeah! Salem frantically tried to dislodge the chain. The dangling pink foot whacked him in the face as he shook his head.

"Another unbelievable coincidence." Setting the box on the table, Zelda smiled at Gabe. "I'm Zelda. And you are?"

"This is Gabe Hawkins." Hilda cooed wistfully. "He teaches music and plays the cello."

"So I heard."

"Where'd you hear that, Zelda?" Gabe asked, genuinely curious. "I just arrived in Westbridge last night!"

"Uh . . ." Zelda brilliantly covered the mistake

with the truth and a playful wink. "The cat told me!"

Gabe winked back. "The cat letting the cat out of the bag, huh?"

"Yes! Something like that!"

"She's such a kidder." Laughing nervously, Hilda shot Zelda a warning look. "She probably overheard us talking by the door."

Concentrating, Salem lowered his head, held the furry foot down with his paw and pulled. The keychain snapped free and the pink foot sailed into the air. It landed in the pile of old clothes still lying on the floor by the back door.

"I confess, I did—" Zelda flinched as Salem leaped onto the table. "Salem! Mind your manners!"

Ignoring her in acceptable feline fashion, Salem sniffed as he quickly read the label on the mysterious box. His eyes widened in astonished wonder and his nose twitched with anticipation! The package contained six samples of a new cat food product called King Kitty. And one of the tins contained caviar! Playing with the furry foot had momentarily distracted him from the morning's obsession, but now that satisfaction was imminent, the craving was overwhelming. Mewing frantically, Salem clawed at the box.

"What's with him?" Hilda asked.

"His wish of the day has been granted," Zelda said with an expression that was both puzzled and disturbed. "There's a can of caviar cat food in that box."

Hilda started. "Too weird."

Zelda cast a guarded glance at Gabe, then stared pointedly at Hilda. *"Exactly* what I was thinking."

"But *I* can't explain it," Hilda said emphatically.

Zelda snapped her fingers.

Gabe froze with his coffee cup poised before his mouth.

"So you didn't conjure up a lucky charm or cast a heart's desire spell?" Zelda asked.

"No! I swear on my witch's honor. I wanted a *real* romantic encounter, remember?"

"Don't look at me!" Salem flinched as Zelda fixed him with a questioning stare. "I lost my powers when Drell turned me into a cat!"

Exhaling, Zelda ran her fingers through her hair. "Well, I suppose all this *could* just be coincidence."

"Can I have my caviar, please?"

"Sometimes reality is stranger than magic," Hilda said. "Now would you mind unfreezing Gabe so I can get on with convincing him that he absolutely adores me? I've only got five hours left!"

"You know," Zelda said cautiously. "You didn't have to *convince* Mr. Kraft to adore you. He just did."

"Willard is an old fuddy-duddy and I never want to see him again." Hilda's eyes blazed. "Is that clear?"

"Perfectly. And I was just getting used to him, too." Sighing, Zelda raised her hand.

"Hey!" Salem hissed. "What about—"

Zelda snapped her fingers, reactivating normal time flow.

Incensed, Salem attacked the box again with a vengeance.

"I'm lost." Taking a hefty swallow of coffee and lowering his cup, Gabe shifted his confused gaze between the two sisters, then focused on the frenzied cat.

"No you're not," Hilda assured him. "I found you."

"Found me? Oh!" Laughing, Gabe helped himself to another cinnamon roll. "I came to the door because I was lost and you found me! That's a good one."

Finally hooking a claw under the sealing tape, Salem pulled the cardboard flap open and dumped the box on its side. A can of King Kitty caviar cat food rolled out. Salem pounced on it.

"Don't you have plans today, Zelda?" Hilda asked hopefully.

"Nothing except dropping those clothes off at Sabrina's school. Which I might as well do now and get it over with."

Oh, no! Reaching out with his paw, Salem snagged Zelda's sleeve with his claws.

"After I feed this obnoxious cat!" Picking up the can, Zelda eyed Salem warily as he retracted his claws, then rubbed up against her.

"A wise decision," Gabe said with an amused twinkle in his eye. "That's the most demanding cat I've ever met."

You've never been around when my litter box is dirty! Salem thought.

The rumble in Salem's stomach increased as he

watched Zelda struggle to pop the lid on the can. It was just dumb luck that they had a mortal guest and he'd have to wait another minute or two because she couldn't use magic to free his prize.

Sabrina stared at Mr. Kraft. "Detention! But—"

"But what, Ms. Spellman?" The vice-principal eyed her coldly.

"I wasn't trying to cheat! I was looking for—another pen and my bag fell off my desk."

"That's not what you told Mr. Rathbone." Perched on the edge of his desk, Mr. Kraft leaned forward slightly. "You told him you were looking for your lucky rabbit's foot."

"Well, I was looking for that, too." Getting more and more mired in the disasterous misunderstanding, Sabrina valiantly tried to dig herself out.

"But there wasn't any rabbit's foot in your bag." Smiling, Mr. Kraft sat back triumphantly and pushed his glasses back onto the bridge of his nose.

"I know. That's the problem."

"No. *These* are the problem." Mr. Kraft waved the folded history notes he had gotten from Mr. Rathbone before he had hauled her into his office.

Sabrina sighed as the weight of the circumstantial evidence buried her. Thinking back, she realized her luck had taken a definitive turn for the worse since she had missed the bus. Even more unsettling was the fact that the magnitude of each successive event seemed to be increasing at an alarming rate. Harvey had seen her having what appeared to be an intimate conversation with Jason and then disappeared before she could explain. Val had agreed to fill in for Benjamin Heller at the rummage sale before she had a chance to ask if she'd work her shift. The whole series of encounters with her friends and Mr. Pool had stolen her half-hour of study time and now this!

"These *are* your cheat sheets, aren't they?" Mr. Kraft pressed.

"No." Speaking calmly and deliberately, Sabrina tried not to sound as nervous as she felt. She was innocent but all too aware that something had gone seriously wrong with her lucky charm. Starting with losing it. *That* made her nervous and acting nervous would just make her look guilty. "They're my study notes. And they only cover the first three pages of the chapter. The test question was about stuff covered at the end."

"But you didn't know that when you made them."

"Does it make sense to have cheat sheets on only ten percent of the material?" The pitch of Sabrina's voice rose in desperation.

Frowning, Mr. Kraft took a deep breath, held it, then exhaled slowly before fixing her with his austere stare again. "Nothing teenagers do makes sense to me most of the time."

"But I wasn't cheating! Those notes fell out of my bag! I didn't even look at them."

"Yes." Mr. Kraft nodded. "Which is why I'm going to be lenient and give you a week's detention instead of suspending you."

"A week!"

"Beginning today. Mr. Pool has the duty this afternoon, I believe."

Sabrina blinked. "But I can't—"

"You should consider yourself lucky that I'm letting you off so easily." Putting the folded notebook papers in his jacket pocket, Mr. Kraft slipped off the desk and returned to his chair. "There're only five minutes left before the bell rings. You can wait in the outer office."

"But—"

Adjusting his glasses and scanning the papers spread across his desk, Mr. Kraft spoke his final word without looking at her. "Dismissed."

Certain that further argument was futile, Sabrina left and sat down on the hard bench in the main school office. Now she had three places to be after school. Detention, the rummage sale, and the Foosball playoffs at the Slicery. Silently bemoaning her devastating ill fortune, she wondered if it was possible to turn herself into triplicates! She'd have to check the book—

And read the fine print!

After leaping to her feet, Sabrina approached the counter.

Standing watch over the photocopy machine that had a notorious and nasty habit of wrinkling emerging copies if the previous page wasn't immediately removed from the tray, the school secretary didn't acknowledge Sabrina when she cleared her throat.

"Pardon me?"

"Just a minute, please." Mrs. Atherton didn't look back but kept her eyes glued to the tray as she carefully took each sheet out of it.

Sabrina didn't have a minute to spare. She had to be at her next class in nine minutes, which was just enough time to pop home, check the book, find the missing lucky charm, and pop back again. Since luck had been with her when she spotted Aunt Hilda's pestle behind the table and had abandoned her before she reached the bus stop, she was sure the enchanted rabbit's foot had fallen out of her bag when she dropped it on the floor.

"I just need a pass for the rest room," Sabrina pleaded.

"In a minute." Mrs. Atherton held up a finger as the duplicating machine slowly and grudgingly produced another copy.

Luck still wasn't giving her a break, either. And the way her luck was going, Sabrina didn't dare leave the office before the bell rang without official permission. She was certain Mr. Kraft would notice her premature absence or another teacher would catch her if she headed to the rest room without a signed, pink pass. Glancing at his door to make sure the suspicious vice-principal wasn't watching, Sabrina pointed at the temperamental photocopy machine. The machine instantly began operating with an efficiency, speed, and accuracy it had not possessed in years.

The secretary flinched as the cranky machine flipped her orginals into the top tray and spat out a neat stack of copies within a few seconds. Shrugging, she removed the copies and turned to Sabrina with a questioning look. "Can I help you?"

"I need a rest room pass, please."

"The bell's going to ring in three minutes."

"Uh—I can't wait. Really."

Unconvinced, the secretary scowled at her.

Sabrina doubled over. "I think I'm going to be sick!"

"No! Don't." Mrs. Atherton quickly scribbled the time and her signature, then ripped the pink pass off the pad and handed it to her. "Hurry!"

Nodding, Sabrina bolted for the door and dared to hope that the hall would be empty so she could immediately pop out!

No such luck.

The school janitor was on his hands and knees, cleaning black scuff marks off the walls.

Sabrina raced for the nearest restroom.

Chapter 6

A split second after entering the rest room, Sabrina popped herself into her bedroom. She half expected to find one of her aunts dusting the furniture or putting away her laundry, even though neither of them was inclined to pursue mortal manual labor to such an extreme. However, if one of them *had* decided to spend a whole day engrossed in mundane household tasks without the benefit of magic, this was bound to be the day. Just about the only things that had gone right since she had awakened in her chair that morning was finding Aunt Hilda's pestle and an empty restroom.

With only six minutes left before third period started, Sabrina dropped her schoolbooks and flipped open the magic book, which was still lying on the bed. Zapping up a huge magnifying glass, she focused on the fine print.

And groaned when she discovered it was written in intricate hieroglyphics totally beyond her comprehension.

"How am I supposed to read the fine print when it's too small to see and written in some weird language no one's used for millennia?" Expressing her frustrations aloud, Sabrina didn't expect a response. She started when the book spoke in a feminine voice that sounded exactly like every nondescript voice on every computerized phone-menu system she had ever heard.

"For large print press one. For language translation press two. For audio press—"

Spotting a series of stars grouped in numerical-order clusters along the upper edge of the fine print section, Sabrina pressed the single star for starters. The stars and the fine print instantly enlarged. However, the text was still written in the mysterious ancient language. She didn't see anything that indicated a way to return to the original menu.

"Now what do I do?" Throwing up her hands, Sabrina glared at the book.

"To review these options press eight. To end this—"

Sabrina quickly counted the clusters and pressed the grouping with eight stars.

"For large print press one. For language translation press two. For audio press—"

Sabrina pressed the two-star cluster.

"To read this passage in Spanish press one. To

read this passage in French press two. To read this—"

Gritting her teeth, Sabrina listened as the maddening book recited the available language options. The joker who had installed the lucky charm fine print menu system had apparently known that some—if not most—of the witches trying to read it would be frantic because their good luck charms had suddenly gone bad. Witches weren't any more patient than mortals when it came to slogging through fine print. And *this* fine print would try the patience of a sleeping slug!

"In English press seven. To—"

Frantic because she was racing the clock, too, Sabrina pressed seven and slumped with relief when the English text appeared in bold print.

Warning: Please be advised that

Bold print that was so big there was only room for one line at the bottom of the page.

"Eeeegh!" Taking a deep breath to calm herself, Sabrina studied the text and the area around it for the key to viewing the rest of the passage. Two small pictures of an ancient scroll rolled around a wooden rod appeared in the left-hand margin just above and below the line of text.

"A scroll. Why not?" Pressing the lower icon, Sabrina smiled as the large text rolled upward.

luck, conjured or natural, is a self-balancing commodity. For every instance of good luck,

there is a countermeasure of bad luck. A witch who conjures a good luck charm to increase her fair share is subject to exponentially escalating measures of bad luck in the event she loses possession of the charm. Whoever holds the charm will have good luck.

Sitting back, Sabrina took a second to let the implications of the fine print sink in. She had lost the charm. Now, not only was she having a streak of bad luck, the bad luck would continue to get increasingly worse until she recovered the rabbit's foot. Considering the magnitude of her misfortune so far, the potential for disaster was alarming.

Quickly scanning the main text again, Sabrina looked for the lucky charm reversal spell. There wasn't one. Or if there was, it wasn't noted on the page.

She briefly considered consulting her aunts, then decided to save that drastic measure as a last resort. She really didn't want to explain that she had made the lucky charm because she had put off her book report and studying for her history test until the last minute. Besides, she knew the lecture on the pitfalls of procrastination by heart and hearing them again wouldn't solve the problem.

But the problem *would* temporarily be solved once the charm was back in her possession.

Rather than popping downstairs and risking a confrontation with her aunts, Sabrina tiptoed to the landing. The sound of Aunt Hilda's soft laughter mingled with a deep and pleasant male voice wafted from the kitchen, the last known location of the renegade lucky charm.

There was no sign of Aunt Zelda.

With only one minute left before the bell rang at school, Sabrina decided she'd be better off returning late with the lucky charm then going back on time without it.

Bracing herself for whatever monkey wrench bad luck might randomly toss her way, Sabrina quietly eased down the stairs. A diversion seemed like her best bet for getting into the kitchen without Aunt Hilda knowing or the man suspecting anything weird was going on.

Taking the first course of action that came to mind, Sabrina rang the doorbell with a flick of her finger, then immediately changed herself into a black cat that looked exactly like Salem. She sprang behind the sofa to hide as Aunt Hilda paused in the doorway between the kitchen and the dining room.

"I'll be right back, Gabe. Don't go away!"

"Don't worry, Hilda. I can't leave yet. There are still two cinnamon rolls left." Gabe chuckled.

Sabrina caught a glimpse of Hilda's guest as he leaned forward. Although he looked to be in his late thirties, he was a hunk even by teenage standards. Aunt Hilda had apparently hit the romantic jackpot!

"Besides, I haven't had a chance to ask you out to dinner tonight."

"Did you say dinner, Gabe?"

53

As Aunt Hilda started to step back into the kitchen, Sabrina rang the doorbell again.

"Hold that thought, Gabe!"

Flattening her cat-self against the couch, Sabrina held her breath as Hilda wandered to the front door with Salem following close behind. When they were past the sofa, she slowly and cautiously moved toward the dining room.

"I thought you were so stuffed you were going to take a nap, Salem." Hilda glanced down at the cat.

"I intend to. After you answer the door. It might be another delivery of exotic delicacies to tempt a refined feline palate."

"Having that caviar cat food Zelda ordered arrive this morning was just a wild stroke of good luck, Salem." Hilda paused to look out the long window by the door. "Doesn't seem to be anybody out there."

Luck? Sabrina stopped dead, remembering how desperately Salem had wanted caviar that morning.

Sitting down at Hilda's feet, Salem cocked his head. "Seems to me that having a tall, handsome, and charming cello player show up out of the clear blue asking for directions was even luckier, though."

Uh-oh. Sabrina glanced at the kitchen. Her window to run in, search the floor, and snag the charm was closing fast, but it couldn't possibly be a coincidence that both Aunt Hilda and the cat had experienced remarkable good luck since she had left for school without it.

Leaning against the door, Aunt Hilda nodded. "I hate to admit it, but you're right."

"Is it even remotely possible that pink rabbit's foot had something to do with it?" Salem asked.

"Possible, yes. But I doubt it." Aunt Hilda smiled. "It doesn't really matter, does it?"

"It does to me!" Salem exclaimed.

Certain that the charm was responsible for their good luck, Sabrina tensed. Where was it now?

"Not to me. Gabe Hawkins is real and we're a perfect match. And *I* didn't use magic to set up our chance meeting." Sighing with contentment, Hilda started back toward the kitchen.

Sabrina crouched behind the sideboard.

Salem padded along behind Hilda, muttering to himself. "Now where did I leave that furry foot? I've suddenly got a craving for lobster with fresh steamer clams on the side."

"You threw it onto that pile of old clothes for the school rummage sale." Pausing in front of the dining room mirror, Hilda pointed at her reflection to fluff her hair and freshen her makeup.

"Oh, yeah!" As Salem bounded for the kitchen, Hilda dashed his hopes and Sabrina's with a single sentence.

"But Zelda just left to take them to the school." Sighing again, Hilda hurried back to the wonderful man fate had dropped on her doorstep.

"No!" Stricken, Salem skidded to a halt. Falling onto his stomach, he covered his eyes with his paws and sobbed. "Blast the rotten luck!"

Ditto! Taking advantage of her feline speed and agility, Sabrina dashed into the living room, bounded up the stairs and into her room. If she hurried, she might be able to intercept her aunt and retrieve the lucky charm before Aunt Zelda delivered the clothes to the gym.

She had a chance, but only if the rabbit's foot was still nestled in the pile.

And if it wasn't?

Sabrina shuddered at the thought. If she didn't get the charm back soon, her escalating bad luck would totally ruin her life by sundown!

Chapter 7

☆

☆

Arms laden with the bundle of old clothes, Aunt Zelda paused just inside the door of the Westbridge High School gym. A long line of people carrying boxes of miscellaneous household items, tools, clothes, books, and toys had formed in front of a table on the near wall. Libby Chessler and Mrs. Quick, Sabrina's math teacher, were sitting behind it writing out receipts for the donations. Other students were unpacking, sorting, and arranging the contributions on racks and tables set up haphazardly around the gym. Confusion, noise, and frenzied chaos prevailed.

Stepping to the back of the line, Zelda sighed. Although she didn't have much hope of ever locating *Dr. Peavey's Basic Principles of Science*, she didn't want to waste time hanging around the school when she could be pursuing the search. Someone somewhere might have a copy sitting on a bookshelf in a living room or tucked away in an attic trunk. She had only barely begun to follow up on a list of secondhand junk stores and thrift shops around the country. She just had to persist until she found the obscure reference book or was satisfied she had tried every means possible before giving up.

"Excuse me." Bending forward, Zelda nudged the man in front of her.

Shifting a rolled-up rug to his other shoulder, the man glanced back and frowned. "Don't get pushy, lady."

"I'm not," Zelda huffed indignantly. "I just want to know if we *have* to wait in this line to drop off our donations."

"You do if you want a tax slip."

"And what if I don't want a tax slip?"

"Beats me." The man shrugged and turned away.

A girl handed Libby a clipboard, then took the cheerleader's place at the table. Remembering that Libby was in charge, Zelda shifted the clothes pile to stop the red silk blouse from slipping off and left the line to follow the girl. Halfway across the gym she tripped over a dangling sleeve and stumbled into a table full of books. The stack on the corner edge toppled to the floor.

"Whoa! Watch it!" A young voice cautioned.

"Sorry." Zelda mumbled as a hand clamped around her arm to steady her. Clutching the bundle tighter, she glanced to the side and saw a face she recognized from the time she and Hilda had turned themselves into teenagers to accompany Sabrina to meet her favorite band. The thin, young man beside her had developed a crush on the "younger Zelda." "Thanks, Gordie."

"You're welcome, Ms. Spellman." The scrawny boy smiled shyly. "I'm surprised you remember me. There were a lot of people at Sabrina's Halloween party." Brightening suddenly, Gordie raised up onto the balls of his feet and waved to someone behind her. "Hi, Gloria!"

Zelda turned as Gloria, a pretty girl with short, blond hair and blue eyes wearing a dusty blue, V-necked sweater over a matching, pleated skirt, walked by carrying a bundle of clothes. The girl didn't even cast a glance in Gordie's direction.

Sighing wearily, Gordie leaned over and picked up an old book with a torn binding. "I might as well be invisible, huh?"

"Maybe she didn't hear you," Zelda suggested gently. The awkward boy obviously had a crush on the attractive girl.

"No. She just doesn't want to be seen talking to a geek." Shrugging, Gordie smiled to try to hide how much the deliberate snub hurt. "But at least now I won't have to work up my nerve to ask her to go to the Slicery for pizza today."

"That's right," Zelda agreed. "There are plenty of other girls who'd probably love to go to the Slicery with you. Ask one of them instead."

"No. I'm going to ask Gloria," Gordie said with grim determination. "I made up my mind to ask her and I have to go through with it. It's a matter of pride, you know?"

"Even if she ignores you?" Puzzled, Zelda eyed Gordie curiously.

"Right! That's why I don't have to sweat it, see?"

"I must be getting old," Zelda muttered. Smiling tightly, she changed the subject. "I see you've got the book table. Who's in charge of old clothes?"

"I think Cee Cee is." Scratching his head with his free hand, Gordie pointed toward the far wall with the book.

Zelda's gaze traveled the length of his arm and stopped. Instantly dropping the bundle of clothes, she snatched the book from his grip. "I don't believe it!"

"No, I'm pretty sure Cee Cee—"

"Forget the clothes!" Grinning with childish glee, Zelda waved the book in the boy's face. "Do you know what this is?"

"Uh—" Squinting through his glasses, Gordie read the title. *"Dr. Peavey's Basic—"*

"Principles of Science! This is fantastic!"

"That book's been out of date for a hundred years," Gordie said seriously.

"I know! How much?"

"Gosh, I'm not sure. Libby hasn't been around to tell me what I should charge."

"Name your price, Gordie!" Zelda snapped, freezing the boy with her no-nonsense stare and possessively clamping the book to her chest. No force on Earth or in the Other Realm was going to deprive her of the prize.

"Well . . ." Gordie exhaled, then shrugged. "A quarter seems fair, don't you think?"

"Yes." Digging into her jeans pocket, Zelda found only car keys. She had been in such a hurry to deliver the clothes and so preoccupied with her seemingly futile search for a book that had been in Westbridge all along, she had left her purse at home. And she couldn't conjure real money. Magically created coins and bills crumbled into metal filings and dust within hours. "Can I borrow one?"

"Sure. It's the least I can do for Sabrina's aunt. Sabrina always treats me like a real person." Pulling a quarter from his pocket, Gordie placed it on the table. "I'll take care of it after the sale officially opens. In fact, I'll even take these old clothes over to Cee Cee for you. Anyone who gets that excited over finding an old book deserves a break."

"You're a doll, Gordie. I'll pay you back."

"That's okay." As Gordie picked up the pile of dumped clothes, a pink rabbit's foot fell out. Palming it, he looked at Zelda hopefully. "Can I have this instead?"

Zelda casually glanced at the furry keychain. "I don't see why not. I'm not even sure where it came from."

"Thanks!" Stuffing the furry foot in his back pocket, Gordie headed across the gym with the clothes. A tuft of pink fur poked through the lower seam of the pocket where the stitching had pulled out.

Consciously choosing not to question her uncanny bit of good luck, Zelda bolted for the exit. She had found *Dr. Peavey's Basic Principles of Science.* Nothing else mattered.

Quickly transforming herself from a cat back into a girl, Sabrina grabbed her books off her bed and popped back to school. This time she emerged in the rest room closest to the gym where the rummage sale was being set up. Given how her luck was running, it was foolish to hope she might beat Aunt Zelda to the gym, but she had to try.

Sabrina stepped into the hall just in time to see her aunt barge out of the gym with a book. She started to wave and shout, but was rudely silenced when Steve Weisel and Randy Johnson ran around the corner and plowed into her.

"Ooof!" Staggering backward, Sabrina couldn't stop herself from falling against the wall or prevent her elbow from busting the glass on the fire alarm. Her jacket snagged on the broken glass and she wrenched her arm as she pulled free. A sharp pain shot through the muscle, but that was the least of her new set of problems.

Aunt Zelda pushed through the outer doors and left without looking back.

Steve and Randy kept running as the shrill sound of sirens screamed through the school.

In the gym Mrs. Quick shouted for calm and ordered everyone outside.

Since Aunt Zelda was gone and setting off the alarm was an expulsion offense, Sabrina didn't stop to think about anything except putting a lot of immediate distance between herself and the scene of the crime.

She popped out.

And into a small dark room that stank of disinfectant.

The janitor's closet. Wrinkling her nose in disgust, Sabrina rubbed the aching muscle in her upper arm. The storage compartment was situated next to the girls' rest room down the hall from the school offices. Frayed nerves and bad luck had obviously thrown off her molecular transference guidance system.

Now ten minutes late for her third period class, Sabrina paused a moment to collect her wits and still her wildly beating heart. In a way, her present predicament could be a lot worse. At least she had popped into a location where no one had seen her mysteriously appear and as far as she knew, no one except Steve and Randy knew she had accidentally triggered the fire alarm. Since they were responsible for shoving her into the wall, chances were good they wouldn't tell.

A quick point relieved the ache in the muscle she had pulled freeing herself from the alarm box. She wasn't about to forfeit the Foosball tournament because of a minor injury, assuming she actually got to the playoffs. Which wasn't likely given how her day was going so far.

Except—

Sabrina brightened suddenly.

When a fire alarm went off, evacuation of the

school building was required by law! And *that* provided the perfect cover for her to ease back into the flow without being obvious about it! *Everyone* was in the halls now, heading for the exits!

Cracking the closet door, Sabrina peeked outside. A steady stream of chattering teens rushed by. Waiting for a break in the crowd, she moved into the current. As she rushed through the outer doors and onto the lawn, she began to relax. Maybe she had successfully diverted this latest bout of runaway bad luck!

Spotting Harvey and Val standing under one of the huge oak trees, Sabrina took a step forward, then stopped when someone tapped her on the shoulder. She glanced back and gasped.

Mr. Kraft glared at her as he held up a student report sheet. Sabrina's name was on it, marked absent from her third period class. "I don't suppose you'd care to explain where you've been, would you, Ms Spellman?"

"The restroom!" Fishing in her bag, Sabrina pulled out the pink paper she had gotten from Mrs. Atherton. "I have a pass!"

Scowling, the vice-principal took the pink slip, studied it for a split second, then glanced at his watch. "This was issued eighteen minutes ago."

"I—uh, felt sick." Grimacing, Sabrina clutched her stomach.

"Uh-huh. Then what were you doing in the utility closet?"

At a loss for a reasonable explanation, Sabrina ran her hand through her hair and sighed in resigned desperation. Since she hadn't recovered the missing rabbit's foot, her streak of bad luck was gaining momentum and nothing she could say would help.

"Your jacket's torn."

"It is?" Sabrina blinked. She had forgotten her sleeve had snagged on the broken alarm casing and she hadn't seen the tear in the dark utility closet.

Peering closely at Sabrina's raised arm, Mr. Kraft blinked and plucked a small shard of glass from the ripped fabric. He smiled triumphantly. "I have a feeling I'll be seeing you in my office again before the day is out."

Sabrina watched in stunned silence as the vice-principal walked away with the evidence to convict her of setting off the fire alarm held firmly between his thumb and forefinger.

Chapter 8

Desperate now, Sabrina stood frozen in place, wondering if there was any defense against the escalating episodes of misfortune.

Only one, she thought as three fire trucks with sirens blaring rolled up to the curb in front of the school.

Get the pink rabbit's foot back.

Somehow she had to get into the gym and find the clothes her aunts had donated to the rummage sale before someone else found the elusive lucky charm.

"Sabrina!" Valerie called.

Fixing her torn jacket sleeve with a quick point, Sabrina turned as Harvey waved. Absently waving back, she noticed Mrs. Quick leading the kids who were organizing the rummage sale out through the door at the end of the building. They ran off to join other friends in spite of the math teacher's effort to keep them together.

Gordie rushed through the scattering crowd, then waved and yelled when he spotted Sabrina. "Have you seen Gloria?"

Shaking her head, Sabrina shouted back. "Sorry, no!"

If she could just find a secluded spot, she could pop into the gym, find the charm and be back outside before Mr. Kraft sounded the all-clear—

"Sabrina!" Val frantically motioned her over.

A disturbed frown clouded Harvey's face when she hesitated.

Taking the opportunity to pop into the gym while it was deserted was an excellent plan—with one exception. Considering how her backfiring luck was operating today, they'd both be so offended by her blatant snub neither one would ever speak to her again.

But that was a chance she had to take. Once she had the charmed rabbit's foot back, her luck would reverse itself and all would be well.

"Hey, Sabrina!"

As Harvey called and started toward her, Sabrina ran for cover in a clump of nearby shrubbery. Stepping behind a tall, flowering lilac bush, she paused to make sure no one was watching.

Harvey stopped dead in his tracks, obviously stunned and confused by her flight and the rejection her actions implied. Shaking his head, he turned and trudged back toward Val, whose troubled expression indicated she felt responsible for Sabrina's strange behavior.

Feeling badly, but too rushed to do anything about her best friend's hurt feelings now, Sabrina popped off the campus and into the gym under the bleachers, which was an unexpected stroke of good luck. She recognized the slippery, red silk blouse that Aunt Hilda had donated lying on top of the pile of clothes on a far table. The missing lucky charm was probably still tucked in the bundle, waiting to be recovered.

Taking a deep breath and clutching her books to her chest, Sabrina sprang out from under the bleachers and dashed across the floor.

Just as Gordie came charging through the gym doors.

"Gloria! Are you in here? Gloria?"

Skidding to a halt, Sabrina scrambled behind a large box. There was no way she could explain to the super brain how she had ended up in the gym only seconds after he had seen her outside. Fortunately, Gordie was totally focused on finding Gloria and hadn't seen her.

Someone whimpered.

"Ohmigosh!" Racing to one of the tables, Gordie lifted the draping to reveal Gloria. He knelt in front of her and gently brushed a stray curl off her forehead. "What's the matter?"

Sabrina stared at the end of the pink rabbit's foot sticking out through a ripped seam in his back pocket.

"Ss-ooo s-scared. I hate fires."

"Well, I uh—don't think there really is a—"

"W-what are you doing here, Gordie?" The terrified glaze in Gloria's blue eyes cleared slightly as she looked up.

Sabrina ducked back out of sight.

Shrugging sheepishly, Gordie pushed his glasses onto the bridge of his nose. "When I didn't see you outside, I got so worried—"

"And you came back into a burning building to rescue me?" Gasping, Gloria knocked Gordie onto his posterior as she flung her arms around his neck. "That is so totally cool!"

Wishing Gordie would just sling Gloria over his scrawny shoulders and rush her to safety, Sabrina peeked out from beneath the table again and saw him flush ten shades of scarlet. She also saw the pink rabbit's foot pop out of his torn back pocket. Although Gordie didn't seem to realize he had lost it, the furry thing was lying in plain view. If she suddenly made it fly through the air into her anxious grasp, both Gloria and Gordie would notice.

"Come on. Let's get out of here." Smiling, Gordie patted the girl's back and urged her to her feet.

Sabrina flexed her finger, preparing to whisk the lucky charm into her hand as soon as Gordie and Gloria were gone.

When Gordie put his arm around her, Gloria nestled her head in the hollow of his shoulder and sighed. "How can I ever thank you for saving me, Gordie?"

"Uh, well—I, uh—" Gordie sputtered, then

took a deep breath and blurted out his question in double time. "Uh, want to go watch the Foosball tournament at the Slicery after school?"

Gloria's head snapped up. "With you? Like on a date?"

"Well, not exactly a date if you don't want—"

"I'd love to." Flashing the astonished nerd a brilliant smile, Gloria almost flattened him again with her unexpected response. "I can't resist a man who's brainy *and* brave."

Quickly recovering from his delighted surprise, Gordie finally began walking her toward the exit. "I don't suppose you like anchovies?"

"I adore anchovies!"

Rolling her eyes, Sabrina raised a finger to snatch the rabbit's foot off the floor, then cringed back as Mr. Kraft burst into the room. Three firefighters wearing full fire-fighting gear followed and fanned out to search the gym.

Foiled again!

"No smoke or flames in here, either." Huffing, Mr. Kraft stopped right in front of the pink lucky charm, folded his hands and assumed a stiff stance. "Just as I suspected."

Not daring to think about what else could go wrong, Sabrina watched and waited.

"Seems like it was a false alarm, all right." Shouldering his ax, one of the searching firefighters approached the furious vice-principal.

A fourth man called in from the hall. "The alarm was triggered out here! The glass on this casing is broken!"

Noticing the shocking pink furry thing on the floor by Mr. Kraft's foot, the ax-carrying fireman picked it up.

"Is that a rabbit's foot?" Mr. Kraft scowled at the charm, then held out his hand. "May I?"

"Sure." The firefighter dropped it into the vice-principal's hand. "You may need a little luck to find the kid who set off that alarm."

"Luck?" Mr. Kraft smiled as his fingers closed over the furry charm. "Maybe. But I have a feeling I'll nail the culprit before the day is out."

"I certainly hope so," the man said. "Every time we respond to a false alarm there's a chance we won't get to a real fire in time to save a building or a life. If you can find this kid and make an example of him—"

"Her." Reaching into his jacket pocket, Mr. Kraft pulled out a handkerchief and opened it to display a sliver of glass.

Inhaling sharply, Sabrina smothered her gasp with her hand. Finding the rabbit's foot near the scene of the crime couldn't possibly connect her with the false alarm. As far as the suspicious vice-principal knew, she had lost her rabbit's foot before her second period history class had started, long before the alarm had been triggered. However, now Mr. Kraft had the good luck of the charm working for *him!* And the shard of broken glass the vice-principal had plucked from her torn jacket sleeve *was* solid evidence that pointed to her guilt!

"We'll need that as evidence. We answer way too many false alarms kids set off every year." Taking the wrapped handkerchief from Mr. Kraft, the firefighter slipped it into his slicker pocket and tipped his hat.

Doomed!

Unless she could get the shard of glass back from the firefighter and the furry pink charm out of Mr. Kraft's iron-fisted grasp! Targeting the ax, Sabrina pointed. The heavy metal head broke off and fell on the floor.

Mr. Kraft jumped with surprise, tightening his grip on the rabbit's foot rather than dropping it.

However, as the startled firefighter looked back, Sabrina pointed at his pocket and unwrapped the handkerchief tucked inside. Then she softly recited an incantation.

"Fired and fused, glass from sand, return to dust at my command!"

Pointing emphatically, Sabrina cast her spell, then winced as a large object on one of the tables fell over with a sharp, metallic *clunk.*

"What was that?" Mr. Kraft's head snapped around and his beady gaze zeroed in on the table. "Who did that?"

Sabrina tensed, torn between trying to get the charm away from the vice-principal and avoiding getting caught inside the school during a mandatory evacuation. Afraid to tempt her rotting luck any further, she wisely decided that sticking around might only make a terrible situation worse. Since the rabbit's foot seemed to have an uncanny knack for changing hands, she was pretty sure Mr. Kraft wouldn't have it for long. Hopefully, it would disengage itself from the vice-principal before he chanced upon something that could *really* make her life miserable. Like proof she was a witch!

Opting out of the gym, Sabrina popped back to the lilac bush and tripped over a tangle of broken branches lying on the ground.

Jason Richards turned at the sound of brittle twigs snapping under her feet.

Just as Harvey came around the far side of the shrubbery cluster.

And she stumbled into Jason's embrace.

Stopping dead again, Harvey blinked and pursed his mouth in a grim, tight line. "Guess not. Sorry."

"Harvey, I can explain—"

"I've got *eyes,* Sabrina!" Scowling with indignation, Harvey turned on his heels and stomped away.

"Harvey! Wait!" Sabrina's bag and books fell on the ground as she pushed away from Jason.

Harvey kept walking.

Jason grinned as he stooped down to pick up Sabrina's things for the second time that day. "You really don't have to keep dropping your stuff to get my attention, Sabrina."

Completely at the mercy of her ill-fated luck, Sabrina just stared at him. Anything she said could and would be used against her.

After sounding the all-clear, Mr. Kraft left the teachers to cope with getting their students back to class and headed directly to his office. Focused on the false fire alarm and the glass shard that linked Sabrina Spellman to the crime, he strode down the hall with a distinct sense of personal satisfaction.

The girl's Aunt Hilda had taken him on a romantic roller-coaster ride that had kept him emotionally unhinged ever since he had foolishly pressed the attractive, but infuriating woman for their first date. That experience had turned into one of the most humiliating and painful moments in his life. Aside from making a shrieking spectacle of herself in the restaurant, she had pepper-sprayed him! Since then, their relationship had been one devastating fiasco after another and had finally culminated in the argument that had sent him home in a rage last Sunday, determined never to speak to or see her again. Now he knew why her old boyfriend, Sonny, had been so anxious to get rid of her. Hilda Spellman was an irrational spitfire with a hair-trigger temper and a mean left hook.

Strange in ways he couldn't quite define, both Spellman sisters were totally beyond the reach of his vindictive authority. Their equally weird niece, however, was not. And *she* had finally made a fatal mistake! One that gave him just cause to expel her.

Glancing at the rabbit's foot still clutched in his hand, Mr. Kraft chuckled as he walked into the school office.

"Mr. Kraft!" The school secretary called excitedly.

"What is it, Mrs. Atherton?" Smiling, Mr. Kraft paused and raised a questioning eyebrow. The woman was practically jumping up and down with glee.

"Remember that request you sent to the Board of Education four months ago?"

Groaning inwardly, Mr. Kraft nodded. That had been the third—no, the fourth request he had sent to the board asking to have the old vice-principal's sign removed from the VP's assigned parking space in the school lot. Given his esteemed position and commendable efforts at Westbridge High, having a sign with *his* name on it seemed like a perfectly reasonable request. However, the expenditure had been denied three times. Four counting today's response.

"What about it?" Mr. Kraft sighed wearily.

"They okayed it!" Laughing, Mrs. Atherton waved an official requisition form printed on blue paper. "You'll have your own sign next week!"

"You're kidding!" Stepping over to the counter, Mr. Kraft set the rabbit's foot down and ripped the blue paper from the secretary's hands. Mumbling as he scanned the page, he laughed aloud when he finished. "You're not kidding!"

"No, sir."

"This is great!" Still holding the paper before his astonished eyes, the vice-principal charged toward his office.

"You forgot your keychain, Mr. Kraft!"

Pausing just inside the doorway, Mr. Kraft glanced back at the pink rabbit's foot he had left on the counter. Realizing he couldn't prove it belonged to Sabrina Spellman and remembering that

75

she had reported her rabbit's foot missing a full period before the fire alarm had been set off, he had no use for it. "Keep it."

Sabrina swallowed hard as she met her chemistry teacher's narrowed gaze. She'd already had one strike against her when she walked into the classroom after the fire evacuation—for not showing up at the beginning of the period.

Strike two had occurred when she had accidentally tripped Leslie Hyashi on her way to her seat and sent the poor girl sprawling in the aisle. Fortunately, the only casualties were Leslie's pride and her own, formerly flawless reputation as a nondisruptive student.

There was no way to avoid striking out.

"What homework?"

Sighing with relief as Mr. Kraft ducked into his inner sanctum and closed the door, Mrs. Atherton rolled her eyes and muttered as she picked up the rabbit's foot to dispose of it.

"At least I won't have to listen to the old grouch complain about not having a personalized parking space every hour on the hour, day in and day—"

"Is there a Martha Atherton here?"

Mrs. Atherton started as a uniformed delivery man walked in and set a bouquet of two dozen long-stemmed roses on the counter. "For me?"

"Are you Martha Atherton?"

Mrs. Atherton nodded. "Who are they from?"

Shrugging, the delivery man removed the card

attached to a long plastic stick and read it aloud in a bored monotone. "Thank you for fifteen wonderful years. Ronald."

"From Ronald!" Mrs. Atherton's face lit up. "This is the first time in fifteen years he didn't forget our anniversary!"

"Congratulations." Dropping the card on the counter, the man sighed and left.

As she reached for the card and sniffed the fragrant blooms, Mrs. Atherton tossed the rabbit's foot over her shoulder toward the lost-and-found box in the corner.

Mr. Pool caught it.

Bolting out of chemistry a split second after the dismissal bell rang, Sabrina raced for the school office. Mrs. Atherton frowned slightly when she came to a breathless halt in front of the counter.

"You're not in trouble again, are you, Sabrina?"

"No. Well, not exactly." Calming herself, Sabrina shrugged. "But I lost a pink rabbit's foot and uh, I was just wondering if you had seen it."

"Why, yes I did. Mr. Kraft left it on the counter and I threw it in the lost-and-found box—"

"Thanks!" Dashing toward the box in the corner, Sabrina stopped short when the secretary finished.

"But Mr. Pool took it."

Dismayed because the charm had eluded her again, Sabrina realized the circumstances could be worse. At least the biology teacher wasn't out to get her like Mr. Kraft. "Does Mr. Pool have a class this period?"

"I believe so."

With less than two minutes to get to study hall on time, Sabrina rushed back into the hall. Since Mr. Pool would be in the biology lab for the next hour, she didn't have to worry that the charm would somehow fall into the hands of someone leaving the school. She could track the teacher and the charm down during her fifth period lunch hour.

Racing into fourth period study hall, Sabrina took a seat in the farthest corner of the room just as the final bell rang.

So far so good.

Taking a deep breath, she closed her eyes to compose herself. If she didn't move or speak to anyone, she might make it through the next fifty minutes without being blindsided by another disaster. She could use the time to speed-read the rest of *The Yearling* and write a report before seventh period English class.

Except the paperback novel was still in her locker.

Chapter 9

☆

Intrigued as he plunged through the lab door ahead of the students, Gene Pool read the note from the librarian again.

> *Drop by the library as soon as you can. Have something to show you. Jane Whitman.*

Although Ms. Whitman probably just wanted to show him another magazine article about the mutant frogs in Minnesota, a topic of recent, idle discussion between them, he didn't want to pass up an opportunity to see her. Especially since he didn't have to make up an excuse for dropping by this time. He had almost asked the attractive, young woman out to dinner on several occasions, but had never quite worked up the nerve. Maybe he'd do it now, when his confidence was bolstered because she had asked to see him! Still upset because his short story had been rejected for the umpteenth time, he really needed a lift. Even if it only lasted as long as it took to walk from the biology lab to the second floor library.

What if she wanted to tell him to get lost?

Mr. Pool paused at the base of the stairs, heedless of the teen traffic swarming around him. He *had* made a habit of stopping by the library to pester the pleasant and attentive librarian with fascinating, scientific tidbits he found on the Internet. She had always seemed interested, but what if he had really been boring her to distraction? To the point where she had to get rid of him or go crazy?

Then again, maybe *she* was upset because he had been so mired in his own creative misery that morning that he had ignored her!

Holding on to that thought, Mr. Pool glanced at Ms. Whitman's note one more time, then folded the paper and stuffed it in his pocket. He grinned when his fingers touched the furry rabbit's foot keychain Mrs. Atherton had tossed to him.

And his hopeful spirits soared.

After all, a rabbit's foot *was* good luck, wasn't it?

"Mr. Pool?" Sabrina called the teacher's name even though it was obvious he was not in the biology lab.

"He took off in a hurry after class." A chubby sophomore boy scrambled to his feet in the back of the room and hitched up his baggy jeans.

"Do you know where he was going?"

"Nope." Lifting a tall stack of books, the boy moved down the aisle between lab tables.

"Did you notice if he was carrying a pink rabbit's foot?"

"Nope."

"You're a big help." Exhaling in disgust, Sabrina edged over to the teacher's desk. The charm wasn't lying on top of it.

The boy eyed her warily as he shuffled to a stop at the front lab table and set down his books.

"What?" Sabrina asked, annoyed. She couldn't casually point the desk drawers open to look inside while the boy was staring at her.

"Mr. Pool isn't here."

"I can see that. What's your point?"

"I think you're acting kind of suspicious." Plopping himself down in the seat, he folded his arms and glared at her stubbornly. "And *I'm* not leaving until you do."

Exasperated and at her wit's end, Sabrina counted to ten to keep herself from turning the obnoxious nerd into a guppy and feeding him to Mr. Pool's giant oscar in the corner aquarium. She also considered her options.

Mr. Pool was really cool—for a teacher. There was no reason why she couldn't just ask him about the rabbit's foot keychain. If he still had it, he'd probably be glad to give it back. If he didn't, she'd at least know what had happened to it before the trail got too cold to follow.

But first she had to find him.

"You didn't happen to notice what direction Mr. Pool took when he left, did you?"

"Nope."

Nodding, Sabrina trudged into the hall. She had been so anxious to catch Mr. Pool before he left the lab that she hadn't stopped by her locker to get *The Yearling.* Finishing her book report hardly mattered now, though. Getting an F for one lousy English assignment was trivial compared to the catastrophe that awaited her the longer the rabbit's foot remained at large.

Mr. Pool was somewhere in the school and she had her whole fifth period lunch break to find him. Starting with the teachers' lounge.

"Mr. Pool!" Jane Whitman's cheeks flushed with excitement when the biology teacher stepped into the library. Wearing a blue blazer and charcoal gray slacks with his hair slightly tousled, he looked even more like an author than a suburban high school teacher today. Her heart fluttered when he greeted her with his charming, boyish smile.

"Hello, Ms. Whitman. You wanted to see me?"

"Yes." Actually, the librarian thought wistfully, she really wanted to see him under more social circumstances. However, Mr. Pool didn't seem to have any interest in her beyond discussing their shared passion for obscure, but fascinating scientific trivia, and she was too shy to make the initial move.

"I have a surprise for you, Mr. Pool."

"Really?" He looked at her expectantly. "What?"

Stepping behind the book checkout desk, Ms. Whitman motioned the curious man to join her. She angled the computer screen to give him a better view, then punched up her personal E-mail account. "I got this from Burt Cassidy an hour ago."

"Burt Cassidy?" Mr. Pool frowned, puzzled. "The editor of *Tales of Time and Space?*"

Suddenly nervous, Ms. Whitman winced. "Yes. I, uh—found your story on the back table and I, uh—I'm afraid I—"

"You read it?" Shoulders sagging when she nodded, Mr. Pool shook his head in dismay. "And you hated it, right?"

"No! I thought it was wonderful. Well-written, good pacing, innovative—" Running out of descriptive phrases, Ms. Whitman got right to the point. "That's why I E-mailed Burt."

"You what?"

Committed, the librarian quickly explained. "Burt and I were in some of the same classes in college, including a writers' workshop and critique group. I was a terrible writer, but Burt always said I had a flare for editing. So I called him to say I thought he had made a terrible mistake when he rejected *The Tachyon Terror.*"

"And?" Mr. Pool's anxious gaze faltered. "No, wait a minute." Reaching into his pocket he pulled out a pink rabbit's foot and held it tightly. "Okay. Now tell me."

Ms. Whitman smiled with amusement. "I received his reply last period. That lucky charm isn't going to change anything."

"What did he say?"

"That rejecting your story *was* a terrible mistake. Somehow your manuscript got shifted into the rejection box." Unable to contain herself any longer, Ms. Whitman giggled. "He wanted to buy it all along! But he couldn't remember who had sent it!"

Dropping the rabbit's foot on the desk, Mr. Pool gripped the edge to steady himself. After slowly scanning the message on the screen, he punched the sky with a victorious fist. "Wahoo!"

"Mr. Pool!" Picking up the rabbit's foot, Ms. Whitman playfully admonished him. "Please keep your voice down. This *is* a library."

"Oh, yeah! Right." Taking a deep breath, the teacher whispered in a jubilant rush. "This is great! If you hadn't written to him, Mr. Cassidy never would have found me! But you did and now I've made my first sale! Want to go out to dinner with me tonight?"

Ms. Whitman gasped.

And Mr. Pool turned pale.

"I'd love to, Gene."

"You would?" Straightening, Mr. Pool cleared his throat to cover his surprise. "Seven o'clock?"

Grinning, the librarian tossed the rabbit's foot back onto the desk, then scribbled her phone number and address on an overdue book reminder pad.

* * *

"Where are you supposed to be, Sabrina?" Mr. Tuttle asked sternly.

"It's my lunch hour." Looking past the gym teacher, Sabrina quickly scanned the interior of the gym. Miraculously, it looked like the rummage sale committee would have everything stacked, hung, and priced in time for the three o'clock opening. However, the biology teacher wasn't in the gym, either. Fifth period was almost over, and Mr. Pool seemed to have vanished into thin air.

"Then shouldn't you be in the cafeteria?"

"Yes, but I've got to find Mr. Pool." Looking desperate, which wasn't hard because she was, Sabrina pleaded with the burly football coach. "It's terribly important."

Shaking his head, the coach dismissed her with a wave and turned away after casting a disgruntled glance at the gym.

"Hey, Sabrina!" Pausing beside her, Val frowned. "Harvey and I waited for you at lunch but you didn't show up. Are you mad at me?"

"No, Val. I'm just having a really bad day."

"I guess! I mean, Jason Richards is a total hunk, but it's not exactly cool to flaunt your passion for somebody else in front of Harvey."

"I'm not flaunting anything with Jason, Val! I just keep running into him! Literally."

"That's *not* what Harvey says." Val shrugged apologetically.

"Great." Frustrated, Sabrina threw up her hands. Even though she was not officially going steady with Harvey anymore, he was her witch's certified true love. The idea that she had hurt him and might lose him because she had foolishly cast a spell without reading the fine print was intolerable. However, she didn't dare try to explain or make amends until the fugitive good luck charm was safely back in her possession.

"He's pretty upset," Val added for good measure. "Harvey, that is."

"Look. I missed lunch because I've been looking for Mr. Pool. I can't explain why, but it's—"

"Mr. Pool?" Valerie blinked. "I just saw him in the library."

"The library?"

"Uh-huh. Cee Cee told me Libby was there. I just wanted to make sure she hadn't changed her mind about letting me work the rummage sale this afternoon."

"Libby's in the library, too!" Without waiting for a response, Sabrina took off. Libby plus unlimited good luck equaled consequences too dire to contemplate!

Slamming her driver's ed book closed, Libby stood up and stretched. However, the exercise didn't quell the shaking in her hands or dispel the feeling of dread that had settled in the pit of her stomach.

If she didn't pass her road test next period, her unchallenged position as *the* social and political force in the junior class would be damaged beyond repair. Getting her driver's license was absolutely essential to the image of confidence and power she had so carefully cultivated and maintained since first grade.

But she was doomed to fail. She couldn't parallel park without bumping into something in a space less than two car-lengths long. However, working with the Department of Motor Vehicles to improve the quality of teen drivers he turned loose on the highways, Mr. Keaton insisted that his students be forced to park in a single space slot. She had it on good authority that the official state testers were more than happy to comply.

Sighing, Libby gathered her books and headed for the exit. As she passed the book checkout desk, she caught Mr. Pool and Ms. Whitman whispering with their heads suspiciously close together. Curious, she paused by the desk.

Both teachers looked up sharply.

"Can I help you, Libby?" Ms. Whitman turned red with embarrassment.

Mr. Pool coughed self-consciously.

"No, I—" Libby's interest in gathering potentially useful information vanished when she noticed the pink rabbit's foot lying on the desk.

Mr. Pool glanced at the clock on the wall, then back at the librarian. "The period's almost over. Guess I'd better get back to the lab."

"Yes. You don't want to be late."

Libby caught the lingering look that passed between the two teachers as Mr. Pool walked away, but she shoved her speculations about a brewing romance to the back of her mind. Her attention was on the furry, pink keychain. It was silly, of course, but she suddenly had the overwhelming feeling that the rabbit's foot might make the difference between passing and failing her road test. The fact that it also matched her pen cap had *nothing* to do with it.

Sighing deeply, Ms. Whitman reached for a stack of returned books, then noticed the rabbit's foot. She picked it up and looked toward the door. "Mr. Pool! You forgot your rabbit's—"

"I'll take it to him!" Snatching the keychain from the librarian's hand, Libby ran after the biology teacher.

And turned in the opposite direction when she reached the hallway.

A numbness settled over Sabrina as she listened to Ms. Whitman.

"Libby took the rabbit's foot back to Mr. Pool, Sabrina."

Nodding, Sabrina headed toward the door, sixth period French, and certain disaster. Knowing Libby would never go out of her way to help someone unless it also benefited herself, Sabrina was also reasonably sure Libby was not taking the keychain to Mr. Pool.

She was reasonably sure her day was about to get much worse.

Chapter 10

Libby stared at the space between cars in astonished wonder.

"This will have to do." Ms. Santini, the DMV officer conducting her road test, sighed with resignation and waved for her to proceed.

Blinking, Libby decided not to question the woman's decision and her incredible stroke of good luck. They had driven around four blocks looking for a suitable spot to test her parallel parking abilities, but the streets were deserted and the best choice was a two-car-length space on Watson Avenue.

Confident that she had aced the test so far, Libby relaxed as she cranked the wheel and eased into the long space. She didn't care whether the pink rabbit's foot in her purse or just a weird quirk of fate had come to her aid. All that mattered was that she would be a licensed driver when she returned to the halls of Westbridge High.

Way!

The French teacher's voice was a background buzz. Sabrina listened to the softly accented drone, but she couldn't concentrate.

Libby had the good luck charm.

And some misfortune of monstrous magnitude was going to befall Sabrina.

It was only a question of when.

And what?

Chewing her pencil eraser, Sabrina watched the clock and waited for the ax to fall.

Lying on the top of the sofa, Salem rolled his eyes and twitched his tail impatiently. Hilda was standing in the open front doorway, still waving good-bye to Gabe. They had been saying their fond farewells for twenty minutes and now that Mr.-Too-Good-to-Be-True was *finally* leaving, he was looking forward to curling up in a comfy, warm lap. Being a cat, there were limited perks in life besides food and catnip. One of the few things he *could* count on was that having met and impressed a man she liked, Hilda would collapse in a joyous swoon on the couch. Given the impact the cello player had made on her, she would probably sit staring dreamily into space for at least an hour.

The phone rang.

Salem tensed with anticipation, expecting Hilda

to stop waving at the empty street to answer it. Zelda was at the library. Now that she had miraculously found *Dr. Peavey's Basic Principles of Science,* she was in a hurry to finish her research and write the paper.

Sighing wistfully, Hilda leaned against the doorjamb.

The phone rang once more.

Noticing Hilda's vacant stare and assuming her impending romantic dinner date had deafened her as well, Salem shouted, "Phone!"

Hilda just smiled insipidly and sighed again.

The phone rang again.

And again. Too late. Zelda's computer was now answering and taking a message.

"Wonder who it was?" Salem muttered. *What if I won the lottery?*

When the phone rang a fifth time, he remembered that Zelda was downloading research files for her writing project and had temporarily disconnected the answer function on the modem. With a bounding leap onto the table behind the couch, he knocked the receiver off the base.

"Spellman residence."

"To whom am I speaking?"

Willard! Salem chuckled, unable to resist a chance to have a bit of feline fun at the vice-principal's expense. Although Hilda had been fond of him before the mysterious incident last Sunday, he still thought Willard Kraft was a goofball.

"This is the cat."

"And *this* is Vice-Principal Willard Kraft at

Westbridge High. I don't know who you are, sir, but I'd like to speak to one of Sabrina's aunts about their niece. Preferably Zelda."

Oops! Was Sabrina in trouble?

Salem hesitated to reconsider his approach. No one would appreciate that he had just given the suspicious vice-principal another weird incident to ponder.

No problem there! Salem chuckled, pleased with the clever and inspired solution that popped into his cunning, cat mind.

"No human is available to answer your call right now," Salem said. "Please leave your name, number and the time you called. Someone will get back to you—"

· "Who is it?" Hissing at the cat, Hilda picked up the receiver and put it to her ear.

"Believe me, you don't want to know. . . ." Salem covered his eyes with a paw.

Opening her mouth to speak, Hilda slapped her hand over the mouthpiece to muffle a stricken gasp.

Salem cringed when she slowly replaced the receiver a moment later. "I didn't know it was him, Hilda! Honest."

"Willard"—Hilda spat out his name as though the sound left a vile taste in her mouth—"thought he was talking to an answering machine and left a message."

"What message?"

Lightning flashed and thunder boomed as a dark

fury replaced the glowing countenance of rapture Hilda had worn since meeting Gabe. She spoke through gritted teeth.

"He said that if Zelda and I want to know *why* he's expelling Sabrina, we should be at the school at four o'clock."

So much for the Spellman lucky streak, Salem thought with a heavy sigh.

At the end of sixth period, Sabrina cautiously left the classroom. Nothing of any consequence had happened. And since Libby had seventh period English, too, Sabrina didn't have to go looking for her to find out what had become of the rabbit's foot. She went directly to class.

Jason Richards caught up with her in the hall and attached himself to her side.

"I'm really in a hurry, Jason." Picking up the pace, Sabrina scanned the corridor for Harvey. If Val was right, he was already convinced she had a major thing for the new boy. She would not be able to explain away a third encounter. Harvey, however, was nowhere in sight.

Jason matched her quickening stride. "There's something I've been trying to ask you all day."

"Okay. Ask. Then I've really got to go." Stopping suddenly, Sabrina whirled to face him. "You've got thirty seconds. I'm having a *really* bad day."

"Gosh, I'm sorry to hear that." Jason frowned with genuine sincerity. "But maybe this will cheer you up."

"What?" Sabrina snapped, then regretted it. Jason had been nothing but nice. In fact, if she wasn't in danger of losing Harvey forever, she might have seriously considered going out with him. "Sorry."

"That's okay. I've got two tickets to the Leopard Spots concert and I thought you might want to go with me."

Sabrina couldn't believe it. Jason had what Harvey wanted most in the world, at least this week. Tickets to the sold-out concert by the hottest band in the country. *It's not fair—*

"I'd love to." Sabrina held up a hand when Jason started to smile. "But I can't."

"Oh. That's too bad." Jason shrugged off her rejection, but his disappointment was obvious. "Don't you like Leopard Spots?"

"No, I think they're totally slammin'." With his awesome looks and cool charm, Sabrina suspected he wasn't used to being turned down flat. "It's just that I already promised to go with someone else— if I win the tickets at the Slicery today."

"What if you don't win the tickets?" A spark of hope flared in Jason's eyes. "The concert's sold-out."

"Yeah, I know, but . . ." Sabrina hesitated, then decided it was better to hit Jason with the truth rather than keep him dangling. "Harvey and I are sort of attached. In a casual kind of way."

"You are?" Puzzled, Jason shrugged again. "Well—"

"Look, I really do have to go." Sabrina cut and

ran for the second floor before Jason could ask more specific questions she couldn't answer quite so honestly. As she hurried down the corridor, though, she couldn't shake a nagging feeling that fate was about to lower the boom.

And she wouldn't see it in time to duck.

Boom number one struck her the minute she walked through the door and spotted Libby. Surrounded by several kids, including Harvey, the cheerleader shrugged nonchalantly.

"The road test was a snap. It never crossed my mind that I wouldn't pass."

Right, Sabrina thought as she edged closer to the group. *That's why you were in a state of total panic this morning.* Libby didn't have a clue that she had had a very powerful luck spell helping her out. More importantly, though, was whether Libby *still* had the charm.

"So you got your license." Nodding, Harvey grinned. "That's super, Libby."

"So why not come to the Slicery after the rummage sale to help me celebrate, Harvey?" Libby asked coyly.

"Sure. I was gonna go watch the Foosball playoffs anyway." Turning to go to his seat, Harvey noticed Sabrina and smiled.

"Hi, Sabrina."

"Hi, Harvey. Look, I—"

"Can't talk now, Sabrina. Bell's gonna ring."

Sabrina blinked. She had just been brushed off by Harvey! Devastated, she almost didn't notice Libby pull the pink rabbit's foot out of her purse.

"Anyone need a little luck?"

"I could sure use some," Jill moaned. "My hairdresser is booked solid next Friday and I've got a totally hot date for the Leopard Spots concert."

Although it seemed like everyone had tickets except her and Harvey, the concert wasn't high on her list of priorities at the moment. If she didn't get the charmed rabbit's foot back, she probably wouldn't be in *any* condition to worry about anything that happened next Friday.

"Hey, Libby!" Sabrina said brightly, holding out her hand. "You found my rabbit's foot! Thanks."

"Your rabbit's foot, Sabrina? I don't think so, freak. This is *Jill's* rabbit's foot." Smiling, Libby tossed the charm to Jill.

"But . . ." Sabrina reached to catch it and missed.

"Cool! Thanks, Libby!" Stuffing the furry pink foot in her bag, Jill slipped into her seat.

"But . . ." Sabrina's protest was cut short when Mrs. Siegler walked in and ordered them all to take their seats. Sabrina kept her eye on Jill and was only vaguely aware of what the teacher was saying.

Until her name was called.

"Let's start with—Sabrina Spellman."

"Huh?" Sabrina's head jerked up. "Me?"

"Yes."

"Uh . . ." Stalling, Sabrina looked around the room, hoping someone would give her a clue. Everyone was watching her and no one gave her a hint. "I, uh—"

"Please, stand to give your report, Sabrina."

"Report? An oral report? On *The Yearling?*"

Muffled laughter rippled through the room.

Mrs. Siegler sighed. "If you don't mind. And please be concise."

No problem there, Sabrina thought as she stood up. She had read most of the classic novel so she might be able to bluff her way through it. Speaking clearly and quickly, she explained how the boy, Jody, had found a fawn after his father, Penney, killed its mother to use her liver on a rattlesnake bite. Ignoring his father's objections, Jody kept and raised Flag.

Sabrina faltered. Penney had just erected a tall fence to keep the grown deer out of the garden when she had stopped reading. She decided to wing it.

"And since the deer couldn't get over the fence, the problem was solved and everyone lived happily ever after." As she sat back down, Sabrina saw Mrs. Siegler frowning at her.

Carol Corning leaned over and whispered. "The kid's Mom shot the deer and Flag died."

Groaning, Sabrina lowered her head onto her arms.

Boom number two descended with a dull thud.

"Obviously, you didn't finish reading the book, Sabrina. So you don't have a written report, either, do you?"

Sabrina shook her head.

The teacher boldly marked her class book, then looked at Sabrina pointedly. "See me after class."

Having totally bungled English, Sabrina spent

the rest of the period trying to solve the after-school problem.

How was she going to serve detention, work the rummage sale, and participate in the Foosball tournament at the Slicery?

She wasn't about to try creating two duplicates without consulting *the book*. There was bound to be some cataclysmic consequence associated with triplicates. So she had to figure out some way to be in three places at once with only two versions of herself to work with.

The answer was so simple, Sabrina almost laughed out loud when the perfect plan sprang into her mind.

She'd make a duplicate for detention where her airhead twin just had to sit and study. How much trouble could the copy get into reading *The Yearling?* None that she could think of. And coming up with three sentences to cover any conversational contingencies in a study hall wouldn't be too hard, either.

Then *she* could pop between the rummage sale and the Slicery without too much difficulty. She'd just have to make a couple of trips to the rest room. There would be other kids at the sale to cover in her absence and the Foosball playoffs didn't start until three-thirty. Once she knew where she was listed on the play roster, she could pop in on time to play her game, then pop out again until the next round—if she won and made the second round.

The only problem with the plan was luck.

If she didn't recover the rabbit's foot before the end of eighth period, anything that could go wrong would go wrong.

But at least she knew where the charm was.

When the bell rang, Sabrina locked onto Jill and followed her into the hall. Another cheerleader and one of Libby's two best friends, Jill wouldn't simply hand over the lucky charm if she was asked for it. Now, however, Sabrina had been driven to a point of such extreme desperation that she was prepared to do just about anything to get the bit of fake pink fur back. Even if that involved using magic and exposing herself as a witch.

Unfortunately, she wasn't going to get the chance before her elective art class started.

"Sabrina!"

Turning at the sound of Mrs. Siegler's sharp command, Sabrina slumped in defeat. Expecting to get a stern lecture about completing her assignments on time, she was surprised when Mrs. Siegler simply handed her a pink hall pass.

Boom.

> *Permission to leave detention. Report to my office at 4:00 for a conference with your aunts.*
>
> *Mr. Kraft, vice-principal*

Sabrina shuffled into the hall in a daze. She didn't know why Mr. Kraft had called her aunts, but it couldn't be good. Although the vice-principal suspected she had set off the fire alarm, he couldn't prove it. Not unless he had found something that incriminated her besides the shard of glass. Then again, she wasn't absolutely positive her spell to turn the glass back into sand had worked. And if it hadn't, Mr. Kraft had all the evidence he'd need to expel her.

Her brilliant plan for being in three places at once wasn't going to work now, either.

There was no way her duplicate could take her place at the meeting.

And she didn't dare miss it.

Chapter 11

By the end of the school day, Sabrina had concluded that the rummage sale wasn't as important as the Foosball tournament, which wasn't as important as the conference with Mr. Kraft and her aunts. However, if everything went according to plan, she might actually be able to cover all her bases. As long as she wasn't scheduled to play her first Foosball round at four o'clock. If there was a conflict, obviously she'd have to forfeit the tournament in order to attend the conference in Mr. Kraft's office.

Looming over all of this was the disquieting realization that salvaging her life from the mess her misguided good luck spell had created was totally dependent on recovering the charm.

But she had not seen Jill since the girl had left English.

First things first, Sabrina thought as she stashed

her books and shoulder bag in her locker. Tucking the pink pass for the four o'clock meeting into *The Yearling,* she held on to the paperback and hurried to the nearest rest room. Her heart sank when she walked in and found Val primping in the mirror. Although she could wait for Val to leave before duplicating herself, she really wasn't in the mood for small talk. But she couldn't ignore Val, either. Val's delicate ego couldn't take getting the silent treatment from her best friend.

"Hi, Val."

Humming, Valerie cocked her head to study her reflection, but she didn't respond.

"Val?"

The girl continued to ignore her.

Apparently, Sabrina thought glumly, *Val isn't in the mood for small talk, either.* In fact, she apparently wasn't in the mood to talk period.

"Okay, Val. What's the matter?"

Val spoke without looking at Sabrina. "I'm really sorry I can't talk to you anymore, but you've been on a social and academic downhill slide to total washout all day and people are beginning to notice."

"So? What does that have to do with you and me?"

"Everything! I finally made a breakthrough with Libby and I can't afford to blow it!"

"What breakthrough?" Sabrina scoffed. "She wants something from you. Believe me, Val. The minute the rummage sale is over, Libby will start ignoring and insulting you again."

"Maybe. Maybe not." Dropping her comb in her bag, Val sighed. "I know I'm being a complete jerk, but I can't help it. I'd give anything if someone really hot would ask me to that Panther Paws concert next Friday—"

"Leopard Spots," Sabrina corrected, rolling her eyes.

"Oh. Yeah." Val shrugged. "Whatever. The point is that nobody's gonna ask me anywhere if everyone thinks I'm a loser because I hang with you, see?"

Sabrina let the comment go. "Selling junk in the gym isn't going to change anyone's impressions of you, Val."

"Yes, it will! Because Libby's running it. Working this rummage sale is the closest I've *ever* gotten to being in with the popular crowd!"

"It's a grunt job!" Sabrina was about to remind her that she was also working the sale, but Val would remember that soon enough.

"It's a chance to fulfill my heart's desire. You wouldn't want me to throw away the opportunity of a lifetime, would you?"

"Honestly, no." Sabrina raised an eyebrow. "But I don't think this is it."

"Thanks. I knew you'd understand." Smiling, Val fled before anyone else came in and found them together.

Shaking her head, Sabrina entered an empty stall. Brushed off by Harvey, shunned by Val, targeted for destruction by Mr. Kraft, and persona non grata with just about everyone else, she had almost totally bottomed out.

Nothing ventured. . . .

"Double, double, toil, and trouble!"

Sabrina flicked her finger, then stepped toward the closed stall door, leaving an exact, but basically brainless copy of herself standing by the toilet. Having already decided what three sentences to program into the duplicate, she handed the smiling dummy her book.

"This is a really great book."

"This is a really great book."

Then she added an affirmative response for any questions that might come up. "Yes, absolutely."

"Yes, absolutely," Sabrina Two mimicked with her plastic smile firmly in place.

And finally something sympathetically agreeable to cover any negative comments. "That can be so annoying."

"That can be so annoying."

Opening the stall door, Sabrina motioned for the duplicate to follow her out. Once her twin had left detention, she'd intercept and absorb her before she arrived in Mr. Kraft's office. "Go to the biology lab and read this book until just before four o'clock. Then show Mr. Pool this pass"—Sabrina tapped the exposed edge of the pink paper sticking out of the book—"and leave. Got it?"

"Yes, absolutely."

"Okay. Get out of here."

"This is a really great book," the copy said as she pushed through the outer door.

With the first phase of her operation taken care of, Sabrina turned her attention to the Foosball tournament. The playoffs didn't start until three-thirty, but the contestant roster had probably already been posted. It would only take her a minute or two to check—

The door flew open. Cee Cee walked in and stopped abruptly.

Seeing the girl's stricken expression in the mirror, Sabrina glanced back. "What?"

"You can't be here," Cee Cee said in a rasping whisper.

"Sure I can. Contrary to what you and Libby would like to believe, you don't have an exclusive claim on this rest room."

"But I just—I just saw you walking down the hall!"

Uh-oh.

"Right, what*ever,* Cee Cee. I'm really down the hall. But now I've gotta go!" Easing by the stunned girl, Sabrina started to push through the door, then paused. "Have you seen Jill anywhere?"

Cee Cee nodded numbly. "On the pay phone by the gym."

"Thanks. See ya!" Bursting out the door, Sabrina ran for the gym. Although knowing the time of her first Foosball round was vital to the plan, she couldn't afford *not* to follow up on Jill, the last known holder of the roving rabbit's foot.

Unfortunately, a woman with an empty shopping bag was using the pay phone in the hall outside the gym—not Jill.

Undaunted, Sabrina ran into the gym and was immediately accosted by a fuming Libby.

"You're late!"

"Sorry." Sabrina scanned the congested room. Although the rummage sale had only been open a few minutes, the gym was already teeming with anxious bargain hunters. Jill was behind a table loaded with dishes and glassware, talking to Robina Yar and waving the furry pink charm.

"Alison isn't here yet, either, and I need someone to cover tools." Exasperated, Libby pointed to the row of central tables Sabrina had hidden under earlier. "Guess you're it."

"Uh-huh. Sure." Without giving Libby another glance, Sabrina headed directly for Jill at the china table on the left.

"Tools are in the *middle,* Sabrina!"

Ignoring Libby, Sabrina strained to hear what Jill was saying as she drew closer.

"Could *not* believe it, Robina! Ronaldo had a cancellation for next Friday just five minutes before I called! It's just too cool!"

Sabrina gasped and stopped short when the rabbit's foot suddenly flew out of Jill's hand. A smartly dressed woman walking by caught it and turned to hand it back.

"I think this is yours." Holding out the pink charm, the woman glanced at a stack of dinner plates, none of which matched. "No, it couldn't be—"

Realizing this might be her best chance, Sabrina sprang forward as the woman set the rabbit's foot down to pick up a plate.

"This is my pattern!" The woman exclaimed. "It was discontinued and no one anywhere has it in stock! I broke one of mine five years ago and had given up hope of replacing it."

"Cool." Jill smiled with lukewarm enthusiasm and picked up the rabbit's foot before Sabrina reached the table. "Guess you don't need this scruffy old thing anymore, either."

"Noooo!" Sabrina squealed as Jill threw the rabbit's foot toward a trash can several feet farther down the wall. Aiming her finger to snatch the charm in midair, Sabrina's point was deflected when Libby grabbed her arm and spun her around.

As Sabrina's arm swung, the interrupted point hit a bucket on the sporting goods display. The metal container jumped off the table and tipped over when it hit the floor, spilling an assortment of used golf balls.

The boy behind the table blinked, then laughed as several customers awkwardly tried to avoid stepping on the little, rolling spheres.

"I need you over *there*, Sabrina!" Libby waved toward the tool tables, then inhaled sharply as a man slipped on a runaway golf ball, lost his balance and grabbed a metal baseball bat rack. The man stayed on his feet, but the bats slipped to one side and fell with a clattering of wood against metal.

Frantic, Sabrina glanced back just as Val bent over behind a table covered with racks and trays of costume jewelry. When she stood up, the rabbit's foot keychain dangled from her finger.

"In a *minute,* Libby!" Pulling away, Sabrina rushed to the jewelry display. "Val! Let me have that rabbit's foot, please."

Appalled, Val stared at her with widening eyes. "You're talking to me, Sabrina! Why are you talking to me here? In front of everyone?"

"Give me the rabbit's foot and I promise" —Sabrina held up her hand—"I'll never speak to you again."

And at the moment, that's a promise I won't find hard to keep.

Incensed, Libby walked up, folded her arms and glared at Sabrina. "Don't do it, Val. That rabbit's foot really is good luck."

"It is?" Obviously pleased that Libby had taken her side, Val dropped the charm into her jacket pocket. "Sorry, Sabrina."

Sagging against the table, Sabrina glanced at the clock high on the gym wall. *Three-twenty!* "I think I'm going to be sick."

Libby stiffened. "Do *not* get sick in here."

"Okay. I'll be right back."

"Never mind. There's Alison." Blowing a wisp of hair off her frazzled face, Libby stalked away.

"Are you really feeling sick, Sabrina?" Val asked with a worried frown.

"I'll be fine after I get a little fresh air. Just do me one favor, Val."

"I can't give you the rabbit's foot. I'd look like a total dweeb if Libby found out." Val's lower lip started to quiver as she dropped her face into her hands. "Sometimes I really hate myself for being so superficial."

Sabrina raised her finger to levitate the rabbit's foot out of the girl's pocket while Val wasn't looking, but before she could point, three elderly women descended on the table.

Sabrina looked at the clock. Three twenty-four.

She didn't have time to wait, but there might be another way to secure the charm without actually taking possession.

"Val!" Sabrina snapped, then softened her tone when the girl looked up. "Just hang on to that rabbit's foot until I get back, okay?"

"Oh, don't worry about that." Val sniffled. "I need all the luck I can get."

And I've got more than I need, Sabrina thought as she headed toward the exit. *Lotsa luck and all of it bad.*

Except that Libby had essentially excused her from the rummage sale and she was going to get to the Slicery before the playoffs started in five minutes.

She was even covered in detention. . . .

Sabrina Two looked up at the nice man called Mr. Pool when he paused by the desk.

"You're in a good mood, considering you're in detention, Sabrina."

"Yes, absolutely."

"In fact, you're the only one in detention today. Besides me, that is." Mr. Pool laughed, then leaned over to look at the book. *"The Yearling.* I hated that book."

"This is a really great book."

"If you like the classics. Personally I don't understand what's so great about it. I don't want to spoil it for you, Sabrina, but the ending is incredibly sad."

"Yes, absolutely."

Mr. Pool's face wrinkled. "You like tragic endings?"

"This is a really great book." Sabrina Two smiled.

"Right. But maybe you should try something a little more current and upbeat. How do you feel about science fiction?"

Sabrina Two hesitated to shift through her limited response options. Only one suited the word *feel*.

"That can be so annoying."

"That's what I thought. You hate it. Just like every snobbish literary critic everywhere. If it's got robots or spaceships and a happy ending, it must be trash."

"Yes, absolutely."

"And you probably think I'm wasting my time trying to write it, don't you?"

"Yes, absolutely."

"Well, let me tell you something, young lady."

Sabrina smiled at the finger the man held in front of her face.

"It just so happens that I sold my first science

fiction story to *Tales of Space and Time* this afternoon. So what do you think about that?"

"That is so annoying."

Mr. Pool's eyes got big. "I really thought I'd get more support from you, Sabrina. Excuse me."

Sabrina Two watched the nice man walk away. Now he was talking to himself.

"Only twenty-eight minutes before four o'clock."

Sabrina Two stopped listening.

Just before four o'clock . . .

Closing the book, she stood up and walked toward the door.

"In three and a half hours I'll be picking up Jane for dinner. Then maybe I'll get some respect!" The man turned his back to look out the window and blew out air again.

Show Mr. Pool that pass and leave . . .

Holding up the book to show Mr. Pool the edge of the pink paper, Sabrina Two left.

Chapter 12

☆

The Slicery was already crowded. All the tables and booths were occupied by kids waiting for the big event to begin. Harvey wasn't there, yet, but the Foosball finalists were standing in a group by the video games and pinball machines. Sabrina shoved her way through the mob to join them.

"Glad to see you, Sabrina." Rod Zinkowski, the assistant manager running the tournament, checked off her name on a clipboard. "Another minute and you would have missed check-in and been disqualified."

"I didn't know that!" Sabrina's eyes widened. Arriving at the pizza place in time seemed suspiciously like good luck. *Maybe the charm's losing its power!* "When am I scheduled to play?"

Rod glanced at the clipboard. "You're up last. Five-fifteen."

"Really?" Brightening for an instant, Sabrina

frowned again. "I don't have to stand here and watch everyone else play while I'm waiting for my turn, do I?"

"No, but don't you want to keep tabs on the competition?"

"No. I think I'd rather meditate. In the girls' room." Smiling, Sabrina casually backed away. "It helps me focus."

"Whatever. Just be here at five-fifteen." Rolling his eyes, Rod called out the names of the first two contestants. "Henry Beagle and Carey Joslin! Front and center!"

Working her way back through the throng of spectators, Sabrina stopped outside the restrooms and sighed with relief. She still had twenty-five minutes before the dreaded confrontation with Mr. Kraft and her aunts, a meeting that would not have seemed so threatening if Aunt Hilda and Mr. Kraft were "on" at the moment.

Frowning, Sabrina wondered as she walked into the rest room. Two girls were checking their make-up in the mirror over the sink and both stalls were occupied. Leaning against the wall, Sabrina considered the implications of recent events while she waited for them to leave.

Nothing really horrible had happened to her since English. She had arrived at the Slicery on time, even though she hadn't known being late for check-in would have disqualified her from the tournament. And her playoff time didn't conflict with the conference in Mr. Kraft's office.

However, *bad* luck had kept her from getting the charm back in the gym.

Jill had called her hairdresser and gotten a Friday appointment minutes after a slot had opened and the china customer had found a rare plate in her discontinued pattern after only holding the charm for a few seconds.

So maybe, Sabrina mused, the brief lull in bad luck was just setting her up to go down in a humiliating defeat in the tournament, which would result in not winning the Leopard Spots concert tickets, which might prevent her from setting things right with Harvey.

Not to mention Mr. Kraft. Although it was possible the vice-principal was using her to wheedle himself back into Aunt Hilda's good graces, it didn't seem likely. *If only I can let Hilda and Zelda know it's all misfired magic, maybe I can escape with only being grounded for a* mortal's *lifetime.*

Two more girls walked into the cramped rest room. Sabrina left.

When she reached the back alley, she had only seventeen minutes left to talk Val into giving her the charm. Without it, her days at Westbridge High might be over a whole year sooner than expected.

Popping back to school, Sabrina raced out of the rest room near the gym.

And right into Mr. Pool's furious presence.

"Mr. Pool!" Smiling tightly, Sabrina brainstalled. How could she possibly explain being outside the gym when the biology teacher had just left her in detention?

"What do you think you're doing, Sabrina?"

"Uh, well—" Sabrina cleared her throat. She had never seen Mr. Pool so angry before.

"Since when do you just get up and walk out of detention without asking permission?"

"I did?" *Uh-oh!* Her double wasn't supposed to leave the room for another ten minutes. Now her practically mindless twin was wandering around the school with no instructions because Sabrina hadn't intercepted her yet—

"I mean, it's bad enough you insulted science fiction, which is *my* favorite genre, and then dismissed my story sale with a flippant remark, but I am *not* going to let you get away with this!"

"You sold your story?" Sabrina grinned, genuinely thrilled for the aspiring writer. "That's great!"

"Can it, Sabrina. You've already made your feelings on *that* subject perfectly clear." Squaring his shoulders, Mr. Pool glared at her.

Realizing her double had somehow given Mr. Pool the impression that she didn't care about his first story sale, Sabrina tried to correct the mistake. "I'm sorry if I sounded negative, but that's not what I meant. Honest!"

"Really?" Folding his arms, the biology teacher rocked back on his heels. "And I suppose you didn't *mean* to walk out of detention when my back was turned, either."

"Uh—I had a pass! To Mr. Kraft's office. I thought you saw it."

"Show it to me now."

"Uh, well—I, uh—" Sabrina winced. Her dum-

115

my double had the pink pass. "I don't have it now, but—"

Mr. Pool smiled. "Well then, since you're so anxious to go to Mr. Kraft's office, I'll escort you!" Scowling again, the teacher pointed down the hall.

Sabrina was about to protest when she saw Jason Richards walk out of the gym twirling the pink rabbit's foot. She didn't know how Jason had gotten the charm away from Val, but he had a crush on Sabrina. No way he'd refuse to give it to her if she asked.

"Jason!"

A bunch of noisy junior high girls came out of the gym at that exact same instant. Their chatter drowned out Sabrina's call.

Jason turned toward the exit without glancing in her direction and disappeared into the outside world.

The charm was beyond reach.

And she was lost.

Hanging her head in despair, Sabrina followed Mr. Pool down the corridor.

After lodging his complaint against her, the biology teacher left Sabrina with Mrs. Atherton, who opened the conference room door and waved her inside. The vice-principal wasn't there, but both her aunts were pacing in agitation.

"Boy, am I glad you're here—" she started to say.

"Mr. Kraft called to say he'd be a few minutes late," the school secretary said.

"I hope he's not going to be too late," Aunt Hilda muttered, annoyed. "I have a few things to say to that—"

Zelda cut her off. "Thank you, Mrs. Atherton." After the secretary closed the door, she turned to Sabrina. "Do you have any idea what this conference is all about?"

"Not really." Sighing, Sabrina glanced at Aunt Hilda. "But whatever it is, Mr. Kraft would probably go easier on me if you'd go out with him again."

"No way!" Eyes flashing, Hilda crossed her arms and stubbornly jutted out her chin. "That stodgy, old stick-in-the-mud geezer can kiss this witch good-bye for good!"

"I can't stand the suspense anymore, Aunt Hilda. What exactly happened between the two of you, anyway?"

"Yes, what?" Aunt Zelda also prodded Hilda to spill the story. "Until Gabe rang the doorbell this morning, you've been making everyone miserable since you had your falling out with Mr. Kraft. You could at least tell us why."

"Gabe? You mean the—" Sabrina caught herself. Her aunts didn't know she had popped home from school while Hilda was entertaining her new friend in the kitchen. "Who's Gabe?"

"A tall, dark, and handsome cello player." Hilda's wistful smile suddenly vanished in an indignant frown. "Who *doesn't* think I'm a ridiculous old maid who's making a fool of herself because I refuse to act my age."

"Mr. Kraft called you a ridiculous old maid?" Zelda started in shock. "That doesn't sound like him. He's always so sweet."

"Maybe to you." Sabrina huffed. "He despises me."

Hilda's scowl darkened. "Just because I *am* hundreds of years old doesn't mean I have to take up knitting and rocking my life away on the front porch. I mean, if he didn't *want* to go roller skating, he could have just said so. He didn't have to resort to insults!"

"I can relate to that." Sabrina dropped into a chair. Her despondent expression drew her aunts' attention.

"You must have some clue why you're in hot water, Sabrina." Hilda looked at her pointedly.

"Yeah. I accidentally set off the fire alarm this morning and Mr. Kraft thinks I did it."

"You just *said* you did." Zelda's eyes narrowed.

"By accident, but I'll never convince Mr. Kraft that it wasn't deliberate."

"Can he prove it?" Hilda asked.

"I don't think so, but I'm not sure." Taking a deep breath, Sabrina launched into an explanation. Having her aunts lecture her about meeting her responsibilites and managing her time more efficiently would be far less cataclysmic than whatever fate bad luck was planning. "It all started when I lost the good luck charm I made this morning—"

"Sabrina!" Both women gasped in appalled unison.

Sabrina rolled her eyes and nodded. "I know, I

know. It was a really stupid thing to do without reading the fine print first."

"That is an understatement!" Aunt Hilda rubbed the back of her neck and sighed.

"You read both fine print sections, though, right?" Zelda asked.

"Both sections?" Sabrina's head jerked up.

"Yes," Zelda said. "You click on *More* following the initial explanation about what happens if you lose it."

"And every witch who has ever made one loses it," Hilda added. "Lucky charms have an annoying habit of wandering off as soon as the current holder experiences a bit of good luck."

"I noticed."

"It's a safeguard to make sure nobody can take unfair advantage of having unlimited good fortune," Zelda explained.

"But," Sabrina continued, "I didn't notice the *More* because I turned the fine print into large print so I could read it."

Both aunts blinked, then simultaneously looked at the clock on the conference room wall.

"When did you cast the spell, Sabrina?" Hilda asked.

"This morning before I left for school."

"What time *exactly,*" Zelda pressed.

Sabrina shrugged. "I don't know exactly, but it must have been around seven-thirty. Why?"

"Better go with seven-fifteen," Hilda told Zelda.

"I didn't wake up until seven-thirteen, so I *know* I didn't make it at seven-fifteen."

"Better to have a calculated margin for error," Hilda explained. "Trust me."

"It's four-oh-three now so . . ." Zelda closed her eyes and did some quick calculations in her head. "That gives her one hour and twelve minutes to deactivate the charm before it's too late."

"Too *late?*"

Zelda nodded. "A good luck charm is only good for ten hours."

"Another built-in safeguard," Hilda explained.

"Right. If you don't get that charm back before five-fifteen," Zelda warned, "you'll have ten years of bad luck."

"Ten years!" Sabrina sat back in alarm.

"And there's absolutely no way to reverse it!" Tilting her head, Aunt Hilda paused thoughtfully, then asked, "What did you use for a vessel?"

"A pink rabbit's foot. Why? Does that make a difference?"

"To you? No." A petulant pout puckered Aunt Hilda's mouth. "But I had it in my apron pocket when Gabe rang the doorbell this morning. So magically created good luck *did* manipulate him into choosing our house when he got lost and meeting him *wasn't* a spontaneous event like I thought."

"I'm sorry, Aunt Hilda."

"Don't be. He's totally charming and gorgeous!"

"And totally irrelevant to Sabrina's problem." Zelda turned to Sabrina. "You've got to deactivate that charm as soon as you find it. Don't wait until the last minute or it will lose itself again. And if it does, your whole young adult life will be ruined."

"Gee, could you make that sound *more* ominous? How do I deactivate it? I couldn't find anything in the book that explains how to reverse the spell."

"That's because you didn't read all of the fine print," Hilda said.

"Here." Pointing at the table, Zelda produced a piece of aged, yellow paper with worn, brown edges and words handwritten in a flowing script. "Put that in your pocket and follow the instructions to the letter when you get the charm back."

Nodding, Sabrina folded the paper and slipped it into her jeans pocket. "Now all I have to do is find it."

"You don't know where the charm is?"

"That's odd," Hilda said. "The one I made to wangle a last-minute invitation to Henry the Sixth's coronation in Paris back in 1431 seemed to get a perverse kick from staying in sight but just" —squinting, Hilda stretched out her arm—"out of my reach."

"Yeah! Mine, too." Sabrina started slightly. "Henry? They crowned a British king in France?"

Zelda shrugged. "He was only ten and not responsible for making the arrangements. The point is that, although Hilda got an invitation, she didn't go to the ceremony."

"No, I didn't. My gown was two sizes too small and I totally flubbed all my spells trying to fix it. So

I had to wear some old rag I pulled out of my armoire. Then the spokes in the coach wheels broke and both horses came up lame."

"And," Zelda added emphatically, "she spent most of the day working as a scullery maid in a tavern because that's where her lucky charm decided to hang out."

"In other words, Sabrina"—Hilda shrugged sheepishly—"lucky charms don't work. They just make things worse."

"Yeah. I made mine because I hadn't studied or finished a book report and the charm didn't help at—" Realizing that she had just confessed, Sabrina looked up sharply. Both women were glaring at her.

"How many times do we have to tell you that magic can't—" Pausing, Zelda breathed in deeply. "Never mind. We can discuss personal responsibility later. Right now you have to worry about locating and deactivating that charm." She looked at the clock. "In the next hour and ten minutes."

"Well, I know that Jason Richards had it fifteen minutes ago"—Sabrina jumped to her feet in a panic—"but he left the building!"

"Any guesses as to where he might have gone?" Hilda asked.

Struggling to stay calm, Sabrina tried to remember if Jason had said anything during the day that might give her a hint. He hadn't. But she had! "The Slicery. I told him I was playing in the Foosball tourna—"

Mr. Kraft's voice suddenly boomed beyond the closed conference room door. "You're *trying* to push the limits of my patience, aren't you?"

"Yes, absolutely."

Sabrina's heart lurched. "Oh no! Mr. Kraft found the duplicate I made to serve my detention!"

Chapter 13

Y ou made a duplicate, too?" Covering her eyes with her hand, Hilda shook her head in disbelief.

Sabrina shrugged. "Well, I couldn't be everywhere!"

"What did you get detention for?" Zelda asked sharply.

"Cheating on a history test, but I wasn't—"

Zelda threw up her hands as the conference room door opened.

"Duck!" Hilda snapped.

Sabrina dove under the long table as the vice-principal ushered the copy out. Sitting in the chair at the end of the table, Aunt Zelda obstructed Mr. Kraft's view of the floor under the table. However, Sabrina could still see most of what was going on through the assortment of chair and people legs.

Still standing, Hilda scowled at the duplicate

with the perpetual grin. "I hope you're happy, young lady."

"Yes, absolutely."

"Is that all you have to say for yourself?" Zelda asked pointedly.

"That is so annoying."

"She's incorrigible." Folding his hands in front of him, Mr. Kraft glared at the copy. "Wonder where she gets that from?"

"Just a minute, Willard." Hilda snapped, obviously struggling to control her temper. Silencing the vice-principal with a piercing look, she turned back at the copy. "Do you have anything else to say?"

Beaming brightly, the copy held up the paperback. "This is a really good book."

Sighing, Aunt Hilda relaxed.

Zelda patted the empty chair beside her and ordered the duplicate to sit. "Sit down, Sabrina. And not another word unless I *ask* you a direct question."

The duplicate sat without opening her mouth.

Clever, Sabrina thought with sudden understanding. Now her aunts knew the three sentences the duplicate had been programmed to say and could phrase their questions accordingly.

"Now, Willard . . ." Hilda faltered when she turned to find Mr. Kraft gazing at her with adoring eyes.

Underneath the table, Sabrina crossed her fingers.

"Hilda . . ." Their longing gazes locked for a

moment before Mr. Kraft came to his senses. Averting his gaze, he nervously adjusted his glasses. "I'm, uh—afraid Sabrina has been, uh,"—clearing his throat, he shifted gears and rattled off the rest of his sentence in his harsh vice-principal's voice— "acting like a petty, self-indulgent juvenile delinquent all day."

"I have not!" Sabrina objected, then clamped her hand over her mouth.

"You have, too." Mr. Kraft turned his stare of authority on the duplicate and began counting off on his fingers. "Cheating, setting off the fire alarm, skipping out of detention—"

"Okay, okay!" Hilda snapped her fingers to draw his attention back to herself. "We get the picture."

"Don't be angry with me, Hilda," Mr. Kraft pleaded, suddenly switching into love-struck mode again. "I'm just doing my job."

"Of course you are, Mr. Kraft," Zelda said gently.

Hilda, however, was not going to let the man off the hook so easily. "I don't *want* to be mad at you, Willard"—Mr. Kraft flinched as she spat out his name—"but you called me a ridiculous old maid!" Hands on her hips, Hilda impaled the vice-principal with another icy stare.

"I didn't mean it! It's just that—"

"Just what?"

Sighing deeply, Mr. Kraft shifted uncomfortably and mumbled. "It's just that I—can't roller skate."

Sabrina covered her mouth again to smother a sudden outburst of giggles.

Mr. Kraft shot the copy another warning look.

"That's enough, Sabrina." Zelda spoke to the duplicate to cover her hidden niece's indiscreet glee, but there was an unmistakable hint of amusement in her tone.

"Well, gee, Willard." Hilda's frosty attitude melted away. "Why didn't you just say so?"

"Because I didn't want you to think I was—*totally* uncool."

"Well, you *are* totally uncool," Hilda said with a mischievous grin. "But on you it's kind of charming."

"Charming?" Cocking his head slightly, Mr. Kraft smiled. "Really?"

"Umm-hmm. But—" Hilda's eyes narrowed with menace. "Don't you *dare* call me an old maid ever again!"

"Oh, believe me, Hilda," Mr. Kraft nodded sincerely, "I won't."

"Excuse me," Zelda interrupted. "But shouldn't we be discussing Sabrina's difficulties?"

Sabrina nodded in silent agreement. Aunt Zelda had waited until Hilda had the ornery vice-principal softened up before broaching the subject of her misbehavior, but time was not an ally. If she didn't find and deactivate the rabbit's foot in the next hour, Val's floundering life would seem like an enchanted existence compared to what hers would become.

"Oh, yeah." Hilda grimaced. "I forgot."

"I really *hate* having to do this," Mr. Kraft said apologetically.

Sure, Sabrina thought. *About as much as I hate hot fudge sundaes with whipped cream and a cherry on top.*

"But I am the vice-principal and disciplining the students is part of my job description."

"Let's begin with cheating," Zelda suggested.

"History test. Second period," Mr. Kraft said stiffly.

"And the teacher caught her?" Zelda gasped.

"Well, no. Not exactly." Coughing into his hand, Mr. Kraft hesitated, then graced Zelda with a smug smile. "That's why I was lenient and only gave her a week's detention."

"But how come she was accused of cheating in the first place?" Hilda asked indignantly.

"She was getting these notes out of her bag." Pulling the folded spiral-notebook papers from his pocket, the vice-principal handed them to Hilda.

"But she wasn't actually reading them?" Zelda asked for clarification.

"No."

Hilda skimmed the papers, then handed them back. "Those aren't cheat sheets anyway. They're incomplete study notes."

"That's what *she* said." Mr. Kraft glanced at the duplicate Sabrina and frowned. "Why are you *still* smiling?" He looked from one witch aunt to the other. "She really is starting to get on my nerves."

Anxious to draw Mr. Kraft's attention away from the duplicate, Hilda touched his arm. "Let's move on, shall we?"

"Certainly, Hilda."

When Mr. Kraft settled his gaze on her again, Hilda continued. "What about skipping detention? Wasn't Sabrina *supposed* to be coming here?"

I have a pass in my book, Sabrina magically sent a thought-gram—express delivery—to Zelda.

Zelda pried the paperback from the duplicate's iron grip, then flipped through the pages. The pink pass fluttered to the floor.

Hilda picked it up. "She has a pass and you signed it, Willard."

"Yes," Mr. Kraft admitted, "I did. But she wasn't supposed to leave detention until four o'clock."

"This says to be *in* your office at four," Hilda argued. "And this pass gave her *permission* to leave detention."

"Seems to me it's simply a matter of interpretation," Zelda observed. "And not a question of deliberate wrongdoing."

"But she left *thirty* minutes early without telling Mr. Pool," the vice-principal explained patiently. "And she didn't come directly to the office. I found her *wandering* the halls like she didn't have a care in the world."

"But, Willard—" Hilda held up a finger to interject. "Since you gave her detention on *suspicion* of cheating based solely on incomplete study notes that she wasn't even reading, Sabrina shouldn't have *been* in detention."

"What's your point?" Willard snapped.

Yeah? Sabrina wondered, equally confused.

Remaining calm and composed, Zelda answered. "Since she shouldn't have been *in* detention, Sabrina can't be found guilty of skipping out on it."

Flustered by the Spellman sisters' convoluted, but oddly rational logic, the vice-principal sputtered. "But—but—"

"I knew we could count on you to see reason." Smiling sweetly, Hilda patted his arm. "So now that the detention problem is settled—"

"We're left with the fire alarm Sabrina allegedly set off," Zelda finished evenly.

"Now that I *can* prove!" Mr. Kraft spun to point a finger at Zelda.

"How can you prove it?" Hilda frowned.

Nodding, Mr. Kraft heaved a resigned sigh. "I found a piece of glass in her torn jacket. Right in the sleeve by her elbow. The local police lab is analyzing the shard and the glass from the broken alarm casing to see if they match. In fact, they should be calling with the report any time."

"What's the standard punishment for that?" An edge of worry had crept into Aunt Zelda's voice.

Sabrina tensed.

"Expulsion. No exceptions, I'm afraid."

"Torn jacket sleeve, you said?" Hilda smiled at the duplicate. "Stand up, Sabrina."

The copy obeyed without hesitation.

"Turn around."

Mr. Kraft's eyes widened in surprise.

"I don't see a tear." Hilda shrugged with a questioning glance at Zelda. "Do you see a tear?"

Zelda leaned over to examine the jacket and shook her head. "No. I don't see a tear, either."

"But it was torn," Mr. Kraft insisted frantically. "I saw it. I pulled a piece of glass out of—"

The conference room door opened and Mrs. Atherton stuck her head inside. "Telephone, Mr. Kraft."

"Okay. I'm coming." The stricken man stared at the duplicate's jacket elbows for another few seconds, then shuffled out of the room shaking his head.

Closing the door behind him, Hilda braced herself against it. "Come on, Sabrina. It's time to pull yourself together."

Sabrina was already crawling out from under the table.

Pulling the copy toward her niece, Aunt Zelda stood back. "Hurry, Sabrina. Poor Mr. Kraft already thinks he's seeing things that *aren't* there. If he walks in and sees two of you, he may never recover from the shock."

"And even though he's a totally uncool and exasperating twerp sometimes, I have gotten rather fond of him," Hilda added.

Nodding, Sabrina breathed in deeply, then stepped back into the duplicate. The double image shimmered slightly as they merged together. She shook her head when the fusion process was complete. "That is so annoying."

"Sabrina!" Zelda sighed. "That wasn't funny."

"Sorry. I think it takes a minute for the programming to erase."

"Well, we've got more immediate problems." Hilda thumbed over her shoulder toward the outer office. "Like that police lab report."

"That's not a problem," Sabrina explained with a satisfied grin. "I turned the glass into sand so there isn't any evidence. I think."

"Sand!" Mr. Kraft's shout was muffled by the closed door.

"So much for the fire alarm!" Crossing her arms, Hilda smiled.

"Yes, but what about Mr. Kraft?" Worried, Zelda nibbled her lip. "He *was* just doing his job and it's not fair to let him think he's losing his mind."

"That depends on your point of view," Sabrina muttered.

"Don't worry about Willard." Stepping away from the door, Hilda dismissed Zelda's concern with a wave of her hand. "I'll take him to dinner tonight and whisper sweet nothings in his ear. He'll forget all about what happened today." She held up her finger to emphasize the point. "And for good measure, he'll be astonished to find out he's a great roller skater!"

"Don't you have a dinner date with Gabe?" Zelda asked.

"Not interested." Hilda shrugged. "Even though Gabe is gorgeous, smart, funny, and talented, he came to our door because Sabrina used *magic* on a rabbit's foot."

"But compared to Mr. Kraft, Gabe sounds like a dream. Are you sure you don't want to reconsider, Aunt Hilda?"

Hilda shook her head. "No. Willard may be middle-aged, paunchy, stubborn, bumbling, and a royal pain, but he showed up on my doorstep completely on his own. Not to mention that he *really* does adore me. For me! Not because I manipulated fate or him with a spell. See?"

"I guess." Sabrina decided it wasn't in her best interests to press the issue. She was much better off when Mr. Kraft and Aunt Hilda were getting along.

Everyone froze when the door opened and the vice-principal entered, shaking his head.

Zelda made a circling motion at Hilda with her finger, indicating they should wrap up the meeting as quickly as possible.

Sabrina glanced at the clock. Four thirty-four. With only forty-one minutes left to find and deactivate the charm, she thought her prospects for the future suddenly looked extremely bleak. *What if Jason didn't go to the Slicery?*

Taking the hint from Zelda, Hilda went directly to the heart of the fire alarm matter. "Was that the police lab?"

"Uh, yes, it was." Staring blankly into space, Mr. Kraft uttered an explanation in a monotone. "The piece of glass in question apparently doesn't exist. The firefighter had sand in his pocket when he got to the lab. I, uh—don't know what to say."

"I do!" Linking her arm through Mr. Kraft's, Aunt Hilda turned him back toward the door. "How about Chinese tonight?"

"I like Chinese."

"Excellent!" Hilda gushed. "I know this great

little place with a dynamite buffet. Then after dinner we can—"

Grabbing Sabrina's arm, Zelda hauled her past Hilda and Mr. Kraft. "I'm late for an appointment. Gotta go!"

"Me, too!" Sabrina waved as Zelda pulled her through the outer office and into the hall.

Checking to make sure the coast was clear, Zelda gripped Sabrina's shoulders. "Get out of here! And find that charm! I do not want to live with a walking calamity for the next ten years!"

Crossing her fingers when her aunt released her, Sabrina nodded. "Wish me luck—no wait! Don't!"

Too late.

Aiming for the back alley of the Slicery, she miscalculated and her molecular transference guidance system glitched again.

She popped into the Dumpster.

Chapter 14

☆

"Yuck!"

Placing the flat of her hands on the heavy lid, Sabrina pushed it open and struggled to stand up. Flipping the top back, she glanced at her knees and the seat of her pants. Gobs of gooey mozzarella cheese and spots of tomato sauce stained the denim. *Easily fixed.* A quick point cleaned her jeans, jacket and hands, but couldn't save her from the humiliation of being found rooting around in the Slicery's garbage.

"Jim Chorgle?" Rod poked his head out the back door looking for a contestant and blinked when he spotted Sabrina. "I thought you were meditating?"

"I am! Or was." Reddening, Sabrina grinned. "There's something very—relaxing about trash. *Nobody* bothers me!"

"That's no surprise. You're up in thirty-five minutes." Rod started to retreat back inside, then looked out again. "Maybe you'd better air out."

"Good idea!"

Shaking his head, Rod ducked back into the restaurant.

Alone in the alley again, Sabrina climbed out of the Dumpster and decided to make double sure the evidence of her disgusting sojourn in the garbage was gone. Closing her eyes, she raised her finger.

> *"Magic finger like a bristle, make this witch clean as a whis—"*

"You are so weird, Sabrina!"

"Cee Cee!" Surprised to see the cheerleader standing in the back door, Sabrina lowered her finger without completing the spell and plastered another inane grin on her face. "How come you're not at the rummage sale? I thought it didn't shut down until five."

"Libby sent me over to save a table. Harvey's meeting her here, you know?"

Although Sabrina didn't appreciate being reminded that her relationship with Harvey was in jeopardy, the topic had distracted Cee Cee from the spell she had almost witnessed. "Well, you won't find an empty table today. This place has been a mob scene since three-thirty."

"Cheerleaders do *not* have trouble finding tables."

"No, but apparently they see doubles a lot." Anxious to find Jason and hopefully the lucky charm, Sabrina barged past Cee Cee. "Excuse me."

Cee Cee wrinkled her nose. "You smell, Sabrina. And you've got mushrooms in your hair!"

"Better watch out, Cee Cee," Sabrina hissed as she went by. "They're contagious!"

"Gross!"

Leaving the cheerleader behind, Sabrina muttered the cleaning chant again as she walked down the hall and pointed before she emerged into the cheering crowd. Hoping the spell had successfully removed the mushrooms clinging to her hair, she scanned the room looking for Jason. He was sitting in a corner booth by himself. Although the table was strewn with glasses and wadded up napkins, she didn't see the pink rabbit's foot.

"Guess I have to ask." Bracing herself, Sabrina squeezed through the crowd. Jostled and blocked, it took her two more precious minutes to reach the booth. But Jason was no longer alone.

Val was sitting beside him.

"Hi, Sabrina!" Grinning happily, Val waved as Sabrina approached the table. "Have a seat. Do you know Jason? He's new at Westbridge and guess what?"

"How come you're talking to me, Val?" Sabrina didn't really want to spoil whatever bit of good luck had made Val so deliriously happy, but the girl *had* told her to get lost. Then, Sabrina reminded herself that finding and deactivating the lucky charm was more important than Val's petty, but forgivable personality flaws.

"Did you two have a fight?" Jason slid closer to Val to make room for Sabrina. "Sit down, Sabrina. Work it out."

Since Jason was the last person she had seen with the fickle foot, Sabrina sat.

"It's all my fault." Sighing, Val shrugged. "I don't blame you for being mad at me, Sabrina. It's just that—whenever a real chance for popularity is dangled in my face, I totally lose sight of everything else. Like, it's programmed into me or something."

"Okay," Sabrina conceded. "But just to make sure I know where we stand—"

Val winced under Sabrina's serious scrutiny.

"Are you still gonna be talking to me when Libby gets here?"

Nodding, Val brightened again immediately. "I stopped caring about what Libby thought the minute Jason asked me to go to the Leopard Spots concert with him! Isn't that great?"

"Super." Sabrina slouched. Now she knew why the lucky charm had abandoned Val. All Val had wanted was a hot date for the Friday night concert. After Jason asked her to go, the charm had been compelled to move on. Her aunts had explained *that* tendency, so that was no mystery, but Sabrina was curious as to how the furry, pink keychain had changed hands and whether or not Jason still had it. "And I bet you gave that rabbit's foot to Jason, didn't you?"

"Yeah!" Val's excited smile faded suddenly. "Oh gosh! I was supposed to hang on to it for you, wasn't I?"

"I know it was a lot to ask, but—"

"Well, it's so weird!" Leaning over, Val whispered. "Jason's father wouldn't let him have the car for the concert. And since Libby seemed so sure the rabbit's foot was good luck, I kind of let him— borrow it."

"I know this is hard to believe," Jason said. "But when I got here and called my dad to tell him I had gotten a date and *really* needed the car—"

"He changed his mind!" Sabrina gasped.

"Yeah!" Jason laughed. "Is that fly or what?"

Sabrina fixed Jason with a narrowed look. "Props. So, what happened to the rabbit's foot?"

Jason sat back with a disgruntled expression. "Cee Cee saw it lying on the table and made such a fuss about how she was positive it belonged to Jill, I let her have— Where're you going, Sabrina? Did I say something?"

"Gotta get ready for my playoff round. Catch ya later." Sliding out of the booth with her gaze still on Jason and Val, Sabrina didn't see the boy balancing three drinks and a plate full of pizza walking by until it was too late.

The boy yelped as he desperately tried to hold on to the plate and keep the drinks from spilling.

Sabrina watched helplessly as most of the soda poured down the front of her white blouse and green velvet jacket. The pizza landed facedown on her boots. Feeling like a magnet for garbage and wishing the charm did not have such a warped sense of humor, she sighed.

The boy had no sympathy for her whatsoever. "I just spent my last five bucks on that stuff. Now what am I going to do?"

Sabrina didn't have any money on her because she had left her bag in her locker. And she didn't have time to stand around arguing because she had to find Cee Cee while the cheerleader still had the lucky charm. *If* she still had it.

Since desperate situations sometimes called for desperate measures, Sabrina pointed into her pocket and pulled out a crisp, new five-dollar bill. It would be tucked inside a bank bag when it turned to dust later today and the short deposit would be chalked up to an error in calculation. Tomorrow she'd slip a real five into the Slicery's till.

"Here you go. Have a nice day." Without waiting for a response, Sabrina plunged into the crowd. When she was safely wedged between kids more intent on what was happening at the Foosball table than anyone standing near them, she executed another deft point to remove the second helping of pizza and soda from her clothes. Then she checked the time.

Four fifty-three.

"And the winner of round six is Jim Chorgle!"

Sabrina saw Harvey walk in the front door as cheers and applause resounded throughout the room.

Keeping him in sight, Sabrina shoved her way

slowly through the crowd. Harvey had no trouble reaching the table in the far corner where Cee Cee was waiting with three empty chairs. Waving the pink rabbit's foot, the cheerleader began to talk excitedly the minute Harvey sat down. With no doubt that something lucky had happened to the girl or that the charm would soon find its way into someone else's possession, Sabrina pressed ahead. However, when she was a mere five feet from her goal, the kids clogging the aisles around the Foosball table wouldn't budge to let her by. Dropping to her hands and knees, she crawled under a table and managed to get close enough to see and overhear Cee Cee and Harvey's conversation.

"All I needed was twenty dollars to get that jacket before the sale ends tomorrow and what happens?" As Cee Cee threw her hands up, she let go of the pink rabbit's foot. It sailed through the air and landed in Harvey's lap. "I glance behind a bunch of cardboard boxes in the alley and find a twenty-dollar bill just lying there!"

"That's nice." Picking up the lucky charm, Harvey smiled tightly. His expression turned grim again when he glanced around the crowded room.

Crouched on the floor, Sabrina wondered if he was looking for her or Libby. She tensed expectantly. If he was looking for her, the power of the charm would make him glance down and spot her lurking under the table—

"Are you Harvey Kinkle?"

Harvey looked up when Rod suddenly appeared at the table.

"Yes. Why?"

"Ryan Laffer didn't show so the five o'clock playoff slot is yours by default."

Sabrina winced. Now that Harvey had gotten a lucky break, the charm would be looking for fresh territory again.

"How totally cool, Harvey!" Perching on an empty stool, Libby tossed her car keys on the table.

"Your dad let you drive his car?" Cee Cee asked.

"Of course." After fixing Cee Cee with a frigid glare, Libby turned to smile at Harvey. "You know, Harvey, the grand prize for winning the tournament is Leopard Spots tickets and twelve pizzas. If you win, we could go to the concert and then throw a totally awesome pizza party at my house afterward."

"I don't want to make any definite plans just yet, Libby."

"Does that mean you're gonna play, Kinkle?" Rod asked. "Or should I track down the next runner-up on my list."

After closing his fingers around the rabbit's foot, Harvey nodded and stuffed it into his pocket and gave his characteristic shrug. "I'll play."

"Your enthusiasm is overwhelming," Rod said. "One minute."

"Right on your heels." Easing off his stool, Harvey sighed and followed Rod toward the Foosball table.

Sixteen minutes and counting. But, at least, Harvey had the lucky rabbit's foot. Now all she had to do was get to him before it jumped ship.

Setting her jaw, Sabrina pointed at the pair of sturdy, jean-clad legs blocking her escape from under the table and intoned softly. "Creepy, crawly things, beware! Move so you're not standing there."

"What was that?" The boy jumped aside and slapped at his leg with his hands. "Something just slithered over my leg."

"Sorry!" Scrambling out from under the table, Sabrina stood up, brushed herself off, then hurried to catch up to Harvey. He was already in place on his side of the Foosball table when she elbowed her way to the front of the crowd.

Standing across from Harvey, Jeff Hughes rubbed his hands on his jeans to wipe the sweat off. He was a good player and a tough opponent.

Nibbling her lip, Sabrina fought the urge to race over and demand the rabbit's foot back from Harvey or risk pointing it out of his pocket while he was playing. When Aunt Zelda had calculated the deadline to doom, she had allowed for a margin of error. Although Sabrina wasn't absolutely certain of the *exact* minute she had made the lucky charm, she was pretty sure it was at least ten minutes after she had awakened at seven-thirteen. She decided to wait. The charm was in Harvey's pocket and in no danger of wandering before he finished his round. Besides, considering his apparent lack of interest in the tournament, he'd need all the luck he could get.

143

Idly moving his rods back and forth to make sure they were all working smoothly, Harvey sighed again.

Remembering how disappointed he had been when he hadn't made the playoffs, Sabrina found his attitude curious. Was he still bummed because he thought she was interested in Jason? Bummed enough to blow a chance at winning tickets to the Leopard Spots concert? That would be too unfair, especially since his worries about Jason and her were totally unfounded.

Wait! Harvey doesn't know that!

"Harvey!"

Harvey's head jerked up and he smiled when he saw her.

But Sabrina didn't have time to say a word.

Rod blew his whistle and dropped his hand to signal the start.

While Harvey's eyes were on her and *not* the Foosball table.

Sabrina winced as Jeff immediately scored the first goal. However, the lucky shot prompted Harvey to spring into action with some measure of enthusiasm. He scored one to tie it. The first player to score five won. Managing his rods with speed and agility, Harvey matched each of Jeff's scores. But, Sabrina realized, if he didn't break that pattern and score his fifth goal first, Jeff would win and move on to the first semifinal round.

When Harvey scored the winning goal, Sabrina leaped into the air with a joyful, "Wahoo!"

"Next up!" Rod barked. "Sabrina Spellman and Juan Alvarez! Three minutes!"

The blood drained from Sabrina's face. She had gotten so caught up in Harvey's game, she had forgotten that *she* had to play at five-fifteen! She barely had enough time to get the charm back. No way she could deactivate it and play in her round, too. Unless the instructions for reversing the spell were really simple.

As she reached for the aged paper Aunt Zelda had given her, Sabrina saw Libby bound out of the crowd to intercept Harvey when he left the Foosball table. If Libby got her hands on the charm, she'd never get it back.

"Harvey! That was great!"

"Thanks, Libby." Flushed with excitement, Harvey laughed as Sabrina rushed over. "Hey! I won."

"I know. We've got to talk. Excuse us, Libby." Grabbing Harvey's arm, Sabrina hauled him back toward the Foosball table, away from Libby and the crowd.

"Pushy much?" Fuming, Libby glared after them.

"Look, Sabrina." Harvey sighed. "I know we decided to see other people, but—"

"I need the rabbit's foot, Harvey. Now. Please."

Harvey frowned, confused by her abrupt response.

"Two minutes, players!"

"Puh-leeze! I know this doesn't make any sense, but I have *got* to have that rabbit's foot!"

Harvey's frown deepened as he reached into his jeans pocket. "Sure. I mean, if you don't care that I'm spending time with Libby, then why should I care about you and Jason?"

"Harvey, I can explain. I just can't do it right now."

After pulling the charm from his pocket, Harvey held it out to her. "Take it. It's not doing me a whole lot of good."

"One minute! Players front and center!"

Just as Sabrina's fingers touched pink fur, a girl stumbled into her. Sabrina stumbled into Harvey and the charm flipped out of his hand onto the floor.

Even with an additional ten minute margin, Sabrina instinctively knew that if she didn't get the rabbit's foot now, she never would. Dropping to the deck, she reached to slap her hand over it.

Unaware, Harvey kicked the charm as he turned to walk away.

Sabrina groaned as the rabbit's foot sailed into the crowd.

☆

Chapter 15

☆

Furious and frustrated, Sabrina pointed.

> *"Lucky charm wherever you be. Get your
> pink self back to me!"*

No more time for subtlety or worrying who
might see.

The charm zipped across the floor and into her
hand.

"Now, folks! Or you forfeit!"

"I'm here!" Closing the rabbit's foot in her fist,
Sabrina got to her feet. No one seemed to have
noticed that the pink furry thing had made a
beeline into her grasp under its own power. She had
the charm, but she was only guessing that she had
until five twenty-three to deactivate it.

"Let's go, Sabrina! Juan!"

Which presented her with a difficult dilemma.

147

To play or not to play.

Darting to her side of the Foosball table, Sabrina looked for Harvey and saw him standing with Libby, and trying not to look at Sabrina.

Then the rabbit's foot quivered in her hand. Startled, Sabrina tightened her grip. None of the many people who had held it over the past several hours had said anything about the rabbit's foot moving. Because it hadn't before, she realized anxiously.

Either the charm's determined efforts to escape had been enhanced because she was a witch.

Or it was already too late.

Rod positioned himself at the end of the table. "Players ready?"

Sabrina and Juan both nodded.

If it was already too late, she had nothing to lose by playing her round—except the round.

But what if she still had those extra minutes?

Rod put his whistle in his mouth and raised his hand.

The smart thing to do was forfeit the game so she could deactivate the charm and end the threat it presented.

But if she did that, she might still lose Harvey. He knew that she knew how much he wanted to go to the Leopard Spots concert. If she quit the tournament and threw away a chance of getting tickets, it would look like she really *didn't* care.

Sabrina breathed in deeply.

Hands flexing on his Foosball rods, Juan stared at her with determined dark eyes.

If it was already too late, she'd lose the round and Harvey no matter what.

But if the deadline was still minutes away, the charm would be lucky for her and she'd win. Then, at least, she'd have some hope of making everything right with Harvey, too.

She decided to gamble on the extra time.

Except she couldn't play Foosball while she was clutching the rabbit's foot in one hand.

Bending over, Sabrina quickly stuffed it into her sock. The furry thing squirmed around her ankle.

Rod blew the whistle.

Concentrating on the ball, the table, and manipulating her rods to block and score wasn't easy with a wiggling rabbit's foot tickling her leg, but Sabrina had come too far to give up without a fight. She focused on flipping paddles.

WHAP! The ball zoomed past Juan's attempts to block and into the net. Slide, block, slide, flip, WHAP. She scored again. And then again when Juan slid his rod forward instead of back giving her a clear shot. WHAP. Juan scored, then attacked the game with a vengeance, but he misjudged the trajectory of the ball and she zinged another one by him. WHAP. Outmatched and shaken, Juan's hand slipped off his rod as Sabrina WHAPPED her winning goal.

"And the winner is Sabrina Spellman!"

The crowd cheered and applauded.

Sabrina shook Juan's hand, but with her leg

shaking and tickling she stumbled against the game table. The charm's struggles were getting stronger and she was sure she wouldn't be able to hold on to it.

One thing, however, was certain.

She had won the round without magic. Had the deadline arrived yet?

Desperate, she pulled the aged instruction paper Aunt Zelda had given her from her jacket pocket.

"First semifinal round in thirty minutes. Kinkle and Dorn first up."

Sabrina's eyes widened in horror as she read the four steps of the ritual she had to perform in order to deactivate the charm.

But she didn't have any choice.

And she didn't have time to find privacy or explain.

"Are you all right, Sabrina?" Harvey asked.

Sabrina looked up. Harvey was watching her with a worried frown and Libby was doubled over laughing. All the other Foosball spectators were staring at her in rapt fascination as she shook her leg to keep the charm from slipping out of her sock.

"Yes, why?"

Might as well give them something really strange to gawk at.

First she had to soak the charm in dark liquid.

Spotting a boy with a soda glass behind Harvey, Sabrina snatched it from his hand.

"Hey! What's the big idea."

Cola. Perfect. Removing the charm from her

sock, Sabrina slipped the wiggling rabbit's foot into the dark soft drink and slapped her hand over the top of the glass.

"Harvey? Could you help me, please?"

Harvey shrugged. "Well, I—"

"You're doing fine making a fool of yourself by yourself, Sabrina." Libby beamed with delight. "You don't need Harvey's help."

The glass began to rattle and Sabrina felt the foot leap against her palm. "Please, Harvey!"

Running his hand through his hair, Harvey considered her. "You're acting really weird again, Sabrina."

"I know. And it's going to get weirder. But it's really important."

"Okay." Harvey sighed. "What do you want me to do?"

Sabrina whispered in his ear.

He shook his head.

"Please? It's . . . it's . . . a good luck charm for the final round thing. Humor me?"

Totally bewildered, Harvey nodded, then stooped slightly and flexed his hands.

A hush of anticipation fell over the room.

Still holding her hand over the cup, Sabrina lowered herself to her knees. Then tipping forward so the top of her head was touching the floor, she counted down. "Three, two, one . . . Now!"

Harvey grabbed her ankles and raised her legs so she was balancing on her head. Sabrina quickly overturned the glass and removed her hand so the top was flush against the floor. Most of the cola and the rabbit's foot remained trapped inside. Then crossing her fingers on both hands, Sabrina quickly counted down again. From ten.

"Ten, nine . . ."

A few kids started to laugh.

". . . seven, six . . ."

Then others joined in with the rapid count.

". . . three, two, one!"

The room became silent again as Harvey lowered her legs. Back on her knees, Sabrina held her breath and lifted the glass. The soda-sopped rabbit's foot rested in a puddle of cola, but it wasn't moving. Not even a twitch.

"What time is it, Harvey?"

"I don't know."

"Five twenty-eight!" Someone shouted.

Dragging herself to her feet, Sabrina turned toward the rest room as the crowd erupted in gales of laughter. A smattering of applause did nothing to lift her spirits.

Five twenty-eight.

"Hey, Sabrina!" Harvey called.

Sighing, Sabrina glanced back as Harvey held up the soggy lucky charm.

"Don't you want your rabbit's foot?"

"Keep it, Harvey. It can't help me now."

And that was too true.

She had recovered the charm and removed the spell.

But she had done it five minutes too late.

Chapter 16

☆

☆

Through all the weird and troublesome events Sabrina had experienced since finding out she was a witch, she had never known such crushing despair.

Ten years of bad luck.

With no way out.

"Sabrina?" Val's voice echoed in the empty rest room.

Sabrina didn't answer. She was sitting braced against the wall in the stall with her feet on the seat lid to minimize the effects of her bad luck. And also because she didn't want any of her friends to suffer by association.

"Sabrina?"

Sabrina sighed as Val bent down and looked under the door.

"You're not speaking to me because you're still mad at me, right?"

"No, Val. I'm just contemplating life at its worst. It's not pretty."

Val's dangling dark hair swung when she nodded. "Oh. Well, that's a relief. Then you must be upset about Harvey. And you should be. He's sitting with Libby."

"Believe it or not Val, he's safer with Libby."

"Boy, you really are bummed, huh? Anything I can do?"

Sabrina shook her head.

"Okay." Smiling, Val waved. "Cheer up, Sabrina. Maybe things aren't as bad as they seem. I mean, Harvey took me out once and all he did was talk about you!"

"Right." Neither Val nor Harvey was aware that she knew about that particular conversation. She had turned herself into a boy and Harvey had confided in Jack Spratsky without realizing it was her.

After Val left, Sabrina found herself thinking about what she had said. Her sweet, but sometimes distracted friend rarely said anything profound, but in this case, Val's lame effort to make her feel better was incredibly relevant to the problem.

Maybe things *weren't* as bad as they seemed.

Having spent the past several minutes wallowing in self-pity, Sabrina latched onto that crumb of hope. There *was* a slim chance she had deactivated the lucky charm before the ten-hour limit was up.

Frowning thoughtfully, she reviewed everything she did that morning from the moment she had awakened in the chair.

She had yelled at Salem, then showered and dressed—with a flick of her finger. Time elapsed: no more than two or three minutes. Then she had apologized to Salem and explained why she was so unnerved and cranky. Another two or three minutes. Then she had frantically searched the room— by hand and by magic—looking for Aunt Hilda's oak pestle. That process had easily taken a few minutes, but she honestly didn't know if it was three or seven. After Salem left, she had gotten the bright idea to make a lucky charm. Another few minutes had passed while she checked the *book,* found the rabbit's foot, and executed the spell.

Tabulating the estimated times on her fingers, Sabrina sat up. The total elapsed time according to her calculations was somewhere between thirteen and eighteen minutes.

A three-minute margin on both sides of the deadline.

Bolstered by this shred of hope, Sabrina stood up. She didn't want to forfeit the Foosball tournament if she had any chance of winning. Besides, the semifinal round might provide the answer to the BIG question.

If she won the round, she'd know for sure that she hadn't been condemned to ten years of bad luck.

Losing the round wouldn't *necessarily* prove anything, though. All the competitors were excellent players and she didn't always win.

But she couldn't stay in the Slicery rest room

indefinitely, either. Sooner or later, she had to face her fate, so it might as well be now.

Harvey and Tate Dorn were just stepping up to the table for the first semifinal round when Sabrina cautiously came out of the rest room hall. Hugging the wall, she edged around the crowd of excited teens to get a better view. Intent on the upcoming game, Harvey didn't notice her.

Which is probably just as well, Sabrina thought glumly. If she *was* a walking bad luck zone, Harvey's game might be affected by something as simple as eye contact with her.

When Rod blew the whistle, Harvey attacked the game. He played the entire round with razor-sharp reflexes, split-second timing, and a ruthless desire to win. Which he did.

Exhaling in relief, Sabrina tensed when her name was called. She was matched with Nancy Spruce. However, as she tried to slip past the crowd to get to the table, the crowd parted to let Tate Dorn through and she was pushed against the wall. The impact sent a jolt of pain through her shoulder.

But her injury wasn't what troubled Sabrina as she made her way to the Foosball table.

A discreet point healed the bruised muscle, but she was all too aware that the incident reeked of perfectly timed bad luck.

Shaken, Sabrina moved into position and realized her hands were sweaty and trembling. A taunt from the audience didn't help her jangled nerves, either.

"Are you going to stand on your head after this round, too, Sabrina?"

The best defense against ridicule was not to let on that it mattered.

Forcing a smile when the crowd laughed, Sabrina took a bow. Whistles and some encouraging applause eased the tension a bit, but not enough to offset Harvey's sad look.

Already rattled when Rod's whistle blew, Sabrina played her best, but it was no contest. Nancy Spruce was an aggressive and talented player and won the round with five goals to her three.

After congratulating Nancy, Sabrina moved into the crowd and headed for the front door. Losing the Leopard Spots tickets was disappointing, but not knowing the status of her luck was worse. However, when Jason intercepted her at the door, she strongly suspected that her luck meter was irrevocably stuck on "tragic."

Harvey was watching.

"Come on back to our table, Sabrina," Jason insisted. "If you leave now, you'll just look like a sore loser. And besides, nothing I say can convince Val you're not still holding a grudge against her."

Since Jason had a point and he wasn't going to take no for an answer, Sabrina surrendered. As he took her arm, she was aware of Harvey's gaze following them. Harvey was still under the mistaken impression that she and Jason were an item. As soon as she could do so without spreading bad luck, she'd go to Harvey and tell him that Jason was going to hear Leopard Spots with Val. If they couldn't be an item, there was not reason not to be friends.

Slipping into the booth with Val, Sabrina asked for a soda when Jason insisted on getting her something. Then she settled back to let events unfold around her. She hated being so passive, but taking action might just tempt bad luck to pull out all the stops.

"It's too bad you lost, Sabrina," Val said.

"Yeah, well. Win some, lose some."

Sighing, Val looked at her narrowly. "How come you're avoiding Harvey?"

"I'm not avoiding Harvey."

"Yes, you are and I think he's noticed."

"He's with Libby," Sabrina said bluntly.

"Hey! Yeah, he is!"

Sabrina looked at Val askance when her friend smiled suddenly.

"Harvey likes me. I wonder if he can convince Libby to give me another chance—"

"Another chance at what?" Sabrina asked curiously.

"Working the rummage sale tomorrow. I, uh— sort of dumped all the jewelry trays when I was packing up today."

When Jason returned with her soda, Sabrina stood up to let him slide into the booth to sit by Val. She kept standing when she realized that Harvey was about to play the last semifinal round. If he won, he'd play against the other remaining contestant in the match to decide the grand prize winner.

Harvey whomped Shirley Mancini.

Standing on tiptoe and straining to see, Sabrina almost *didn't* see Randall Emerson smack Gordie when he threw his fists in the air to hail Harvey's victory. Gordie's arm flew up, launching the slice of pizza on his plate over his shoulder.

Sabrina leaped to the side and gasped as the pizza landed facedown—on the floor!

Stunned, Gordie looked back. "Gosh, I'm sorry, Sabrina. Randall hit me—"

"Thank you, Gordie!" Giving the surprised boy a hug, Sabrina laughed. "It missed me!"

"Well, yeah." Gordie sighed. "But now I have to fight my way back through this crowd to get Gloria another piece."

Although she still couldn't be one hundred percent certain the bad luck had lifted, Sabrina now had good reason to think that maybe she *had* deactivated the charm before the doomsday deadline.

There was only one true test to find out for sure.

"Thanks for the soda, Jason, but I've got to go watch Harvey play the final round. See ya!"

Here goes nothing, Sabrina thought as she barged into the jam of teens eagerly jostling for position to watch the deciding match. Her spirits rose another notch when she found a spot near the front with a clear view of the table.

Wiping his hands on his jeans, Harvey met Jim

Chorgle's steady gaze. Both boys grabbed their rods as the ref raised his hand. Taking a deep breath, Harvey glanced up and looked right at Sabrina.

Smiling, Sabrina held up two sets of crossed fingers. "Good luck!" *For* both *of us,* she thought.

Harvey blinked—

"Players ready?" Rod asked.

Then Harvey immediately turned his full attention to the table.

The whistle blew.

WHAP! Harvey reacted without hesitation, scoring his first goal before Jim even realized the game had started.

Watching the ball and mentally making every move with Harvey, Sabrina gritted her teeth as Jim countered his next shot with a solid block and whacked the ball toward his goal. Harvey not only blocked the ball, he WHAPPED it. Score number two.

Rising to the challenge, Jim scored next after a series of volleys. Unflustered and focused, Harvey played with a fervent will to win. WHAP.

Breathless as the closely matched boys battled it out, Sabrina tensed when Jim sunk his fourth goal, tying the score.

With his jaw clenched and his gaze riveted on the table when the final ball rolled into play, Harvey skillfully blocked two of Jim's shots, then— WHAP!

The crowd went wild before Rod could officially

announce Harvey Kinkle as the Slicery Foosball Champ.

Sabrina was pushed back as the mob surged forward to surround the winner. She caught a glimpse of Harvey as he was swept into the crowd and propelled across the room toward the corner table where Libby was laughing and cheering. Casually pointing at the packed bodies blocking her way, Sabrina rushed to catch up when the mob parted before her.

Spotting her just as he reached Libby's table, Harvey waved. "Hey, Sabrina!"

Frowning as Sabrina eased out of the crowd, Libby called out. "Harvey! Over *here.*"

Harvey ignored the cheerleader.

Planting herself in front of him, Sabrina grinned even though her insides were knotted with apprehension. "That was a great game, Harvey."

"I think this helped." Harvey pulled the damp, brown stained rabbit's foot from his pocket and dropped it in Sabrina's hand.

Wrapping her fingers around the charm, Sabrina just nodded.

Harvey smiled tightly. "Guess I'll be going to the Leopard Spots concert after all. I just wish you were going with me."

The bad luck bubble hanging over Sabrina's head burst.

"Why wouldn't I be?"

Puzzled, Harvey frowned. "I heard Jason say that he was going to ask you."

"He did. I turned him down."

"You did?"

Sabrina shrugged. "Yeah. I'd rather go with you. That is if you—"

Harvey cut her off. "But what if I hadn't won the tickets?"

"Well, I'd rather be *not* going with you, too!"

Relieved and thrilled, Harvey laughed. "Then I guess it's a date."

"A date!" Libby's eyes flashed as she wedged herself between them. "You asked Sabrina to go to the concert, Harvey? What about me?"

"I told you I didn't want to make any definite plans, Libby."

"And making a date with *her* isn't definite?" Libby's eyes widened with disbelief as her gaze fell on the rabbit's foot Sabrina was holding.

Harvey shrugged. "I changed my mind."

"Well, thanks a lot!" Snatching the rabbit's foot from Sabrina's hand, Libby picked up her car keys and stormed out the door.

"Libby's gone," Sabrina quipped. "Want to celebrate with Val and Jason and me?"

"Uh—" Harvey hesitated.

"What?" Sabrina waited. Harvey had had the rabbit's foot in his pocket when he won the tournament and she had been holding it when he asked her to go to the concert. And now that Libby had it, he had suddenly become reluctant to be with her?

What if the charm was still working?

Leaning closer, Harvey whispered. "You're not going to do anything weird again, are you?"

"You mean like stand on my head by an over-turned glass with my fingers crossed counting back-ward?"

Harvey nodded.

"No." Sabrina held up her hand. "I promise."

Taking her hand, Harvey smiled as he started toward the back booth where Val was frantically waving at them. "What was that all about anyway?"

"Uh—well, I just wanted to show you that" —Sabrina grinned impishly—"I'm a fool for you, Harvey Kinkle."

"Do me a favor, okay? Next time just *tell* me."

"You got it."

Suddenly the loud, unmistakable sound of a car crashing into something solid resounded through the Slicery and the streetlight just beyond the door went dark.

"Oh, no!" Libby wailed from the street outside. "My car!"

Sabrina smiled.

The rabbit's foot was just an ordinary carnival doodad once again.

And luck in Westbridge was back in balance.

About the Author

Diana G. Gallagher lives in Minnesota with her husband, Marty Burke, three dogs, three cats, a cranky parrot, and a guinea pig called Red Alert. When she's not writing, she spends her time walking the dogs, puttering in the yard, playing the guitar, and going to garage sales looking for cool stuff for her grandsons, Jonathan, Alan, and Joseph.

A Hugo Award–winning artist, Diana is best known for her series *Woof: The House Dragon*. Dedicated to the development of the solar system's resources, she has contributed to this effort by writing and recording songs that promote and encourage humanity's movement into space. She also loves Irish and folk music and performs at local coffeehouses and science fiction conventions around the country.

Her first adult novel, *The Alien Dark*, appeared in 1990. She and Marty coauthored *The Chance Factor*, a STARFLEET ACADEMY VOYAGER book. In addition to other STAR TREK novels for intermediate readers, Diana has written many books in other series published by Minstrel Books, including *The Secret World of Alex Mack*, *Are You Afraid of the Dark*, and *The Mystery Files of Shelby Woo*. She is currently working on original young adult novels for the Archway Paperback series, *Sabrina, the Teenage Witch*.

What would *you* do with Sabrina's magic powers?

You could win a visit to the set, a $1000 savings bond and other magical prizes!

GRAND PRIZE
A tour of the set of "Sabrina, The Teenage Witch" and a savings bond worth $1000 upon maturity

25 FIRST PRIZES
Sabrina's Cauldron filled with one Sabrina, The Teenage Witch CD-ROM, one set of eight Archway Paperbacks, one set of three Simon & Schuster Children's books, and one Hasbro Sabrina fashion doll

50 SECOND PRIZES
One Sabrina, The Teenage Witch CD-ROM

100 THIRD PRIZES
One Hasbro Sabrina fashion doll

250 FOURTH PRIZES
A one-year subscription of Sabrina, The Teenage Witch comic books, published by Archie Comics

Name_____

Address_____

City_____State_____Zip_____

Phone(_____)_____

Sabrina, The Teenage Witch™ Sweepstakes Official Rules:

1. No Purchase Necessary. Enter by mailing the completed Official Entry Form or by mailing on a 3" x 5" card your name, address and daytime telephone number to Pocket Books/Sabrina, The Teenage Witch Sweepstakes, 13th Floor, 1230 Avenue of the Americas, NY, NY 10020. Entries must be received by 7/1/98. Not responsible for lost, late, damaged, stolen, illegible, mutilated, incomplete, not delivered entries or for typographical errors in the entry form or rules. Entries are void if they are in whole or in part illegible, incomplete or damaged. Enter as often as you wish, but each entry must be mailed separately. Winners will be selected at random from all eligible entries received in a drawing to be held on or about 7/7/98. Winners will be notified by mail.

2. Prizes: One Grand Prize: A weekend (four days/three nights) trip to Los Angeles for two people (the winning minor and one parent or legal guardian) including round-trip coach airfare from the major airport nearest the winner's residence, ground transportation or car rental, meals, three nights in a hotel (one room, occupancy for two) and a tour of the set of "Sabrina, The Teenage Witch" (approximate retail value $3500.00) and a savings bond worth $1000 ($US) upon maturity in 18 years. Travel accommodations are subject to availability; certain restrictions apply. 10 First Prizes: Sabrina's Cauldron filled with one CD-ROM (a Windows 95 compatible program), one set of eight Sabrina, The Teenage Witch books published by Archway Paperbacks, one set of three Simon & Schuster Children's books and one Hasbro Sabrina fashion doll (approximate retail value $100). 25 Second Prizes: Sabrina, The Teenage Witch CD-ROM published by Simon & Schuster Interactive (approximate retail value $30). 50 Third Prizes: Sabrina doll (approximate retail value $17.99). 100 Fourth Prizes: a one-year subscription of Sabrina, The Teenage Witch comic books published by Archie Comics (approximate retail value $15). The Grand Prize must be taken on the dates specified by sponsors.

3. The sweepstakes is open to legal residents of the U.S. and Canada (excluding Quebec). Prizes will be awarded to the winner's parent or legal guardian if under 18. Any minor taking a Grand Prize trip must be accompanied by a parent or legal guardian. Void in Puerto Rico and wherever prohibited or restricted by law. All federal, state and local laws apply. Employees of Viacom International, Inc., their families living in the same household, and its subsidiaries and their affiliates and their respective agencies and participating retailers are not eligible.

4. One prize per person or household. Prizes are not transferable and may not be substituted except by sponsors, in event of unavailability, in which case a prize of equal or greater value will be awarded. All prizes will be awarded. The odds of winning a prize depend upon the number of eligible entries received.

5. If a winner is a Canadian resident, then he/she must correctly answer a skill-based question administered by mail.

6. All expenses on receipt and use of prize including federal, state and local taxes are the sole responsibility of the winners. Winners may be required to execute and return an Affidavit of Eligibility and Release and all other legal documents which the sweepstakes sponsor may require (including a W-9 tax form) within 15 days of attempted notification or an alternate winner will be selected. Winner's travel companions will be required to execute a liability release prior to ticketing.

7. By accepting a prize, winners or winners' parents on winners' behalf agree to allow use of their names, photographs, likenesses, and entries for any advertising, promotion and publicity purposes without further compensation to or permission from the entrants, except where prohibited by law.

8. By participating in this sweepstakes, entrants agree to be bound by these rules and the decisions of the judges and sweepstakes sponsors, which are final in all matters relating to the sweepstakes.

9. The sweepstakes sponsors shall have no liability for any injury, loss or damage of any kind arising out of participation in this sweepstakes or the acceptance or use of the prize.

10. For a list of major prize winners, (available after 7/15/98) send a stamped, self-addressed envelope to Prize Winners, Pocket Books/Sabrina, The Teenage Witch Sweepstakes, 13th Floor, 1230 Avenue of the Americas, NY, NY 10020.

™ Archie Comic Publications, Inc. © 1997 Viacom Productions, Inc. All Rights Reserved.